TWO TIME LOSER

A SAMANTHA TRUE MYSTERY

KRISTI ROSE

Vintage Housewife Books

PO BOX 842

Ridgefield, Wa 98642

www.kristirose.net

Publisher's Note: This is a work of fiction. Names, characters, places, and incidents are a product of the author's imagination. Locales and public names are sometimes used for atmospheric purposes. Any resemblance to actual people, living or dead, or to businesses, companies, events, institutions, or locales is completely coincidental.

Cover Design © 2022 Strong Image Editing

Edited by: Paula Proofreader/Gemma Brocata

Two Time Loser/ Kristi Rose. -- *1st edition*

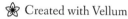 Created with Vellum

As always:
To DHM. You are everything

To Luke: You were the best dog ever and gone far too soon. I miss you everyday.

To you, Reader: 2021 was not an easy year. Because of that I tried to find laughter. And I hope you find it in these pages, too. Thank you for reading. Thank you.

In Memory : My brother Todd, my Aunt Rose, my friend James, my grandma Jessie, my Uncle Gary, my friend Amy and sweet girl, Madeline. How lucky I was to have you in my life.

BOOKS BY KRISTI ROSE

Samantha True Mysteries- Laugh out loud twisty mysteries

One Hit Wonder

All Bets Are Off

Best Laid Plans

Caught Off Guard

Two Time Loser

A Liars Island Suspense (written under pen name Robbie Peale)

Perfect Place

Campus Murder Club- The dead are not forgotten (Episodic Mystery on Vella)

Campus Murder Club

The Wyoming Matchmaker Series- Whether marriage of convenience or star crossed lovers, everyone earns their happily ever after in this series.

The Cowboy Takes A Bride

The Cowboy's Make Believe Bride

The Cowboy's Runaway Bride

The No Strings Attached Series- A flirty, fun chick lit romance series

The Girl He Knows

The Girl He Needs

The Girl He Wants

The Girl He Loves

The Meryton Brides Series- A wholesome romance series with a Pride and Prejudice theme

To Have and To Hold (Book 1)

With This Ring (Book 2)

I Do (Book 3)

Promise Me This (Book 4)

Marry Me, Matchmaker (Book 5)

Honeymoon Postponed (Book 6)

Matchmaker's Guidebook - FREE

The Second Chance Short Stories can be read alone and go as follows:

Second Chances

Once Again

Reason to Stay

He's the One

Kiss Me Again

or purchased in a bundle for a better discount.

The Coming Home Series: A Collection of 5 Second Chance Short Stories (Can be purchased individually).

Love Comes Home

THURSDAY, NEWSPAPER OFFICE

"STELLA," DAD PLEADED AS HE LOOKED AT HIS coworker over his glasses.

She put up a hand. "Don't, Russ. I don't want to hear it." Her voice quivered as if she were barely holding on.

Dad's brows shot up, and the cup of coffee I'd brought to my lips hung in limbo for a moment as I studied the woman who'd worked with Dad for decades now. She was like a second mom to me. And for a woman on the eve of her wedding, she looked ready to come undone. In all my years of knowing Stella MacInerney, I'd only seen her like this three times.

Each time was when she'd lost a husband. Stella had the unfortunate history of marrying men who dropped dead within a year of saying I do. She was an active woman who picked unhealthy men, believing she could make them healthier. Sadly, many had been unhealthy for too long.

"All I was going to say, Stella, was that you don't have to be here. I know you have a lot to do, and I can manage the paper by myself for a few days," Dad said.

Stella glanced at me. Her eyes narrowed as she tried to work out my dad's ulterior motive.

I cut to the chase. "You look overwhelmed, and that's not like you."

She heaved a heavy sigh while glancing around the bullpen, the open space that made up the center of the paper. Back in its heyday, this was where the reporters would've worked. But now it was just Dad and Stella and a handful of freelancers.

Today, Dan, my dad's IT guy who managed the website and all things digital, was banging away on his laptop, upgrading something or other.

Stella wagged a finger at him. "Last time we did an upgrade, the system crashed and we were scrambling. That's why I feel overwhelmed. I can't handle going through that again right now. I wish we would have waited to do this upgrade."

"No crashing is going to happen today," Dan argued. "I've tested and retested. And I wish you had a little more faith in me, Stella."

She snorted. "Oh, like you have faith in me. I overheard Chuck say you placed a bet that Tom wouldn't last three months. I don't think betting on the lifespan of my future husband is a funny sport, Dan Dix."

Dan had the good sense to look ashamed. "I didn't start the betting, and I didn't know it was going on until Chuck asked me if I wanted in on it. Besides, It's not just Tom's longevity we're betting on. There are odds on you, too, and Sam."

Stella looked confused. "Me? Why?"

I sat up straighter. "Me?"

Dan tapped away on his keyboard, giving Stella a quick glance. "I don't know the specifics, Stella. Something about how his wife died mysteriously. No one knows anything about her. As much as people like Tom, they wonder if you're not the one who will be eighty-sixed this time."

Stella gasped and clutched her hands to her chest. "That's just awful. People are heinous."

Dan continued to work. "Like I said, I didn't start it, just heard about it."

Stella looked at me and Dad. I put up my hands in surrender. "I didn't place a single bet, and I knew nothing about the bets on you." I was insanely curious about the bets on me, however.

Dad did the same, hands up in denial. "Me neither. So callous." He shook his head in disgust. Outside of this one event, Dad was known to put a few dollars on the latest town bet. Stella's upcoming nuptials were all anyone in town could talk about. And I was telling the truth. I hadn't placed a single bet. But Precious had, and I'd put in my two cents. I was giving Stella and her karma the benefit of the doubt and believed this one would stick.

I cleared my throat. "So, Dan, what kinda bet is out there on me?"

He pecked away at the keyboard. "Just if you and Leo will be each other's plus-one."

"That's a dumb bet," I said. Never mind that Precious and I had belabored this topic to death last night. Question was, did I want to be a plus-one?

Stella shrugged. "Well, it's really about whether you two will do something other than give each other smoldering looks from across the room."

Dad snort-laughed and quickly covered his mouth and pretended to cough.

I made a face that I hoped portrayed my disgust. "We don't give each other smoldering looks. We sit on my balcony and drink beers. We have a professional relationship and a blossoming friendship."

Stella gave me a kind smile. "I didn't bet on you either. When you're ready, you'll know, and I would never be so insensitive as to ignore that." She shot glares at the guys.

Dad cleared his throat. "Speak of the devil. Leo's coming." Dad jerked his head toward the large window at the front of the office. Sure enough, Leo was taking large strides toward the building. He looked to be on a mission, a frown on his face.

"Maybe he's going to Chuck's," I said. Chuck's was the name of the market next door.

Dan stood up and said, "I've got two dollars that he's coming here to talk to Sam. Maybe to ask her to the wedding."

I wadded up a piece of paper and tossed it at him. "I'm already going to the wedding, dumb-dumb. I'm Stella's maid of honor."

He paused mid-sit. "Shouldn't it be matron of honor? You were married before."

I wagged a finger. "Except it wasn't a legal marriage, so technically, I was never married. Therefore, *maid* of honor."

Dan dropped into his chair with a huff. "Lost that bet," he mumbled.

The bell above the front door jingled as Leo entered, and I went to meet him.

"Hey," I said.

He was dressed in his uniform. His sleeves rolled up. His eagle tattoo glaring at me. Like it always did.

"Is there somewhere we can talk privately?" He looked around the office, nodding at Dad, Stella, and Dan back in the bullpen.

"Sure, we can use Dad's office for a second." I waved for him to follow me. Once in the room, I closed the door behind us.

Leo stuck his hands on his hips, ducked his head, and sighed. "I have a favor to ask, and I need you to not pepper me with questions afterward."

I grimaced. "You know me. That's going to be hard." I was half joking.

He looked up at me through his brows. "I need you to dig deep with this one. It's not something I want to talk about."

I leaned against Dad's desk and crossed my arms. "I'm so curious. Just ask, let's go from there."

He grunted and began pacing the room. "It's not fair for me to ask you to do something blindly. I just hate rehashing something from the past." He seemed to be talking more to himself than me. I let him make a few turns around the room before interrupting him.

"What is it you need me to do?"

He stopped and faced me. "I need you to be my date at the wedding."

Because he hadn't come in and simply asked me to the wedding, I knew this request was loaded with a story I desperately wanted to hear. "You know the town is betting on whether we'll go together to this wedding."

He closed his eyes and groaned.

"And why do I feel like this is because you need cover?"

He looked at me. "I dated Stella's wedding planner in college."

I pushed off the table and sprang toward him, clasping my hands with excitement. "Oh my word! You can't just tell me that and leave me hanging. You dated in college?"

"Ha, ha."

"I mean, in high school you dated Penny Bradshaw and Tulani Whitehorse, but those were casual. Nothing more than a handful." I wagged my finger in his face. "But this, you asking me to be your plus-one, is because there's been more than a handful of dates. How long?"

He swallowed and looked away. "Two years."

I gasped. "You dated a girl two years and kept it a secret from even Hue? Your own brother?"

He shrugged. "It wasn't serious. It was college."

I shook my head and moved back to sit on Dad's desk. "You're a moron. I bet it was serious to her."

He met my gaze. "Yeah, I learned that the hard way. She knew I was coming back here, and I knew she wanted to live large in Seattle. I thought it was a no-brainer that our relationship was just casual dating. But can we not talk about it anymore? I need you to tell her we're, you know..."

"Dating?"

"Engaged."

I burst out laughing. "What? Engaged?"

He shrugged.

"Oh, I see. Because you dated her for two years and ended it, she'll rightly believe that dating doesn't mean a whole lot to you. But engaged. That's the real deal."

He grimaced "So, you in?"

I held up my bare ring finger. "I'm the kinda girl who needs something big and sparkly."

He grinned. "No, you're not. But you're the kinda of girl who deserves something big and sparkly. Just tell her it's getting sized. So, we good?"

I nodded. "I can't wait to tell Hue."

He rolled his eyes and moved to the door.

"Hey, how did she get to be Stella's wedding planner if she lives in Seattle?"

He turned to me. "I'd like to know the answer to that too."

"You know, that frown you were wearing when you came in has turned upside down. I'm glad I could be of assistance."

"Oh, shut up," he said with a chuckle.

We exited the office, and he waved to the gang. "See you all later at the rehearsal."

I waited for Leo to leave before I said to Dan, "Better go place a bet on me and Leo being a plus-one, because that one's about to come true."

"Already did," Dan said.

Dad and Stella looked at me in question.

"I'll explain later. Quick question, Stella. How did you find your wedding planner?"

Stella said, "Online. One of those wedding sites where you put in what you're looking for, and people contact you. I was surprised she was willing to travel to do the planning, but she was. She's lovely."

"I'm sure she is, " I said, tongue in cheek.

Dad interrupted. "I was just telling Stella that bets, website upgrades... neither of those are reasons for her to be here when she could be doing what I'm sure is one of the million things on her list."

I agreed. "Dad's right. The rehearsal is in a few hours.

You have time to go do something—anything—else. Maybe a quick massage, if you don't have anything on your list."

Stella liked to keep lists. She was so good at it, she would make them for others as well. Over the years, I've had my fair share from her.

She crossed her arms. "Tom and I have a couple's massage scheduled tomorrow before the wedding." She raised her hand to stop any comments. "There will be a curtain between us so he can't see me. I'm no dummy. I don't play fast and loose with superstition. I'll take any and all luck I can get. And there are only two things on my list for today. Both will be taken care of before the rehearsal." She faced me. "I think it's great you and Leo are going to the wedding together. You need to move on."

Everyone looked at me. I was holding my coffee again, so I took a sip. I made it a long sip.

"Samantha. I would really love to see you out dating again," Stella said.

I put my mug down and groaned. "Dating again and bringing a date to a wedding are two different levels in a relationship."

Dad cleared his throat. "I agree with what you just said. But I agree with Stella. Time to get your feet wet again."

I raised my brow. "Feet wet? Is that what the kids are calling it these days?" It was a stupid joke, but I did that when I was nervous. And talking about relationships made me nervous. "I'm just not sure I'm ready. So let's just accept a plus-one at the wedding as a good first step, please?"

Stella crossed her arms and studied me. "Perhaps a little part of you blames yourself for picking Carson, who was such a superb con man."

I shrugged. "Well, it's a little hard to trust my radar. I

mean, I bought into Carson hook, line, and sinker." If I were to repeat my mistake, wouldn't that make me a two-time dummy?

"You can trust Leo," Stella said. Never one to mince words.

I had no response to her statement. She was right. I knew I could trust him. But love and friendship are different. And weirdly, trusting him with my life was easier than trusting him with my heart. Leo was, after all, a guy who'd essentially shunned me in high school even though his kid brother is one of my best friends, and our paths crossed all the time.

I picked up my mug and took another long and leisurely sip. Dad chuckled. Stella was cut off from saying anything further when her phone rang. She stepped away to answer it.

Dad said under his breath, "You can run, Sammy, but you can't hide. You're gonna have to answer these same questions soon enough. This isn't the Regency period where a widow was expected to mourn for a year. Everyone here knows what Carson did; no one wants to see you unhappy."

"I'm not unhappy. Weirdly, I'm happier than I've been in a long time, before and during Carson." And it was the truth. After all, I had this new fabulous life of being a PI because of Carson.

Stella had moved to her desk, fifteen feet away, so when she gasped, everyone in the room paused and looked her way. "Oh no! This can't be happening."

Dan said, "Jeez, I hope it's not what I think it is. I'm curious, though, to know if anyone had placed a bet today."

"Dan, that's awful. I'm sure nothing's happened to Tom." I rose and moved to Stella. Dad was right behind me.

She hung up the phone, leaned against her large desk,

and began yoga breathing. This was Stella trying to get control.

"Stella?" Dad asked. "Everything okay?"

She shook her head. "No, Russ."

Dad and I glanced at each other, him likely afraid to ask about Tom as much as I was.

"It's the girl I hired to smudge the wedding garden and pavilion before the rehearsal tonight. She can't do it. She had a family emergency. How am I going to find someone on short notice?" She covered her face with her hands. "The bets, and now this. It's like love is always fighting me."

I rubbed her back. "I think I can find someone to smudge on short notice, Stella. Let me take care of this for you."

She looked up from her hands, moisture in her eyes. "Who?"

I jerked my head in the direction of the coffee shop, Java Magic. "I think this is something right up Lark Ogilvy's alley." Lark was relatively new in town and the owner of the coffee shop. Her specialty was coffee combinations brewed to help with people's auras. "And if she can't do it, I'm sure between Leo, Precious, and I, we can find someone who smudges."

Stella nodded, sucked in another deep breath, and slowly blew it out. Afterward, she patted my cheek. "I think I freaked out there for a moment. It's not like me to not be able to solve a problem. It's just that this wedding means so much to me. I want everything to be perfect."

Next to her, Dad leaned against the desk. "Which is why you shouldn't be here. We're a distraction. There has to be something else you can do."

Stella smiled. "Actually, the custom garden statue I had made for Tom is ready, and I want to bring it to the rehearsal.

He'll get a good laugh. It's two garden gnomes hugging with a heart between them. It stands about this tall." She held her hand up from the floor to three feet.

Tom owned a landscaping business. Gardens were his jam, but gnomes were not something I'd seen in any of his designs.

Stella continued. "It was delivered to Bruce's house, and I wanted to do it up a bit with little white lights and such. Maybe I should go get it and do that." She glanced at her watch. "Then I can bring it to the rehearsal."

"I think you have enough time before we have to meet at the venue," I said. "Do you need help moving it?"

She shook her head. "I'll call Bruce and tell him my plan. Oh, but can I borrow LC? The statue won't fit in my car." Stella drove a MINI Cooper.

I dug in my pocket and handed her the keys to LC, my temperamental Wagoneer named after pioneers Lewis and Clark, because both they and my Wagoneer had seen some adventures. "I just got the brakes fixed. They're a tad touchy. You barely have to tap them to make them work."

She grabbed me in a hug. "Thank you." Then gave me the fob to her car.

I added. "And I'll go to Lark and see if she'll smudge. We'll meet you at the rehearsal."

Stella clasped her hands in delight. "Sounds like a plan."

We sent her on her way, glad to see her happy once again. I waited until she was out of sight before turning to my dad, a lingering question on my mind.

He held up a hand. "Before you ask; no. I don't know how Tom's first wife died. They moved here after it happened, and he's never talked about it."

Stunned, because I got my insatiable curiosity from him,

I asked. "How is that possible? You know everything. What did she say when you asked?"

He shrugged. "I didn't ask. It's none of my business."

"Do you think Stella knows?"

"I'm going to have to trust that she does."

I bit my lip. Conversations like this seemed to come back to haunt me.

2

THURSDAY AFTERNOON

Lark was more than excited about smudging Stella's rehearsal and wedding venue. She needed no convincing to leave her shop in the capable hands of her one employee.

We met at the gazebo outside the reception hall at the Wind River National Wildlife Refuge and Park, where Stella's events were to take place.

Lark followed me to the gazebo and pulled out two wads of rolled sage. They looked like giant joints. With a long, fat braid down her back and flowy skirt and peasant top, Lark, holding two oversized joints, looked very normal. This woman knew who she was, and for a second, I was envious that she was so comfortable and confident in her skin.

"Two?" I said. "As far as I know, this place isn't haunted or anything."

"I brought extra, just in case." Lark beamed and lit one of the sage joints. "You never know what's lurking in the shadows." She chuckled.

I followed her as she waved the smoke all around the

gazebo. Taking her time and, not that I know anything about smudging, looking like she was doing a good job.

"This means a lot to Stella," I said.

"I'm glad I could help." She cut her eyes to me. "It's been hard getting to know people in Wind River."

I grimaced. "Yeah, I'm sorry about that. I think because the previous owner of the coffee shop wasn't a great person, folks in town have been cautious about getting to know you."

Lark waved the joint in the air. "I get that. Logically. But it's still hard. I remind myself to be patient."

I wasn't looking to make new friends; I didn't have any place for them and I'd be a terrible one. Because when bad guys came after me, they typically came after my friends too. But I felt bad for Lark. Who cares that she always tried to read your aura and that was annoying. She was a nice person.

"You know, we're practically neighbors. You live above the coffeehouse; I live above the paper. We could hang out sometime."

Lark looked at me with wide eyes. "That's very nice, Samantha, but don't take this wrong. I don't want to hang out with you. A black cloud of trouble follows you everywhere. My luck, I'd absorb all the collateral damage from your trouble."

There was too much truth in her words to take offense. I shrugged. "Any chance you could sage that cloud and get rid of it?"

She chuckled. "I wish." But she waved the sage around me anyway. We grinned at each other.

"Speaking of dark clouds. Here comes trouble," Lark said over my shoulder.

I turned around to find a strikingly beautiful woman

walking toward us. She was the same height as me, and her hair was the same strawberry blonde as mine, though she had chunkier blonde highlights. Trendier than me. I was too lazy to do more with my hair than keep it trimmed.

"Who is that?"

"The wedding planner, I think," Lark said. "She was in the shop the other day and introduced herself. Mariah, I believe. You know, from behind, you two could be sisters. I almost mistook her for you until she turned around. From the front, you look nothing alike. Just the hair. Had I thought about it at the moment, I would have realized there is no way she could be you. Look at how her hair curls around her shoulders. I don't think I've ever seen you with your hair down. It's always in a ponytail or sloppy bun."

I patted my bun self-consciously. "I thought sloppy was in."

Lark pointed to my temple. "And then there was that shaved part where you had those stitches from when you got blown up. It's growing in better now, but for a while there"— Lark gave a whistle—"it looked rough."

"Thank you." My tone was purposefully droll.

"But this one?" Lark gestured with her chin. "This one is up to no good. She's *made* her dark cloud. She's invited it in and snuggled up to it."

With surprise, my eyes went wide, and I glanced back at the wedding planner. Leo's old girlfriend. She wore a silky jumper that hugged her curves in all the flattering places. Precious was going to love the outfit.

"Hi." Mariah waved as she got closer. "What's going on here?"

I was wearing a dark green skirt with a tiny vines-and-flowers pattern. I stuck my hands in the skirt's pockets, taking a moment to appreciate such a thing. Against my waist I could feel the little pouch I'd safety-pinned to the skirt that held a handcuff key and a small pocketknife. Two very essential tools. I was confident Mariah's onesie didn't have a pouch with a handcuff key or a tiny knife.

"We're smudging the gazebo and moving to the reception hall next. It's something Stella really wanted," I said.

"And you are? Because I'm the wedding planner and I think I would know what Stella wants."

Lark moved to stand slightly behind me. "Samantha's the maid of honor and has known Stella forever, right, Sam?" She waved the joint in Mariah's direction and tried to blow the smoke toward her, but the wind shifted it away.

Mariah took a staggered step and caught herself. "You're Samantha?" She looked me up and down as she slowed her stride.

I nodded. "Stella will be a little late. She stopped by to pick up her groom's gift."

Mariah waved a hand toward the parking lot. "But I saw her car."

"I drove it. She has mine."

"Oh, excuse my manners. I'm Mariah Quessenberry." She extended a well-manicured hand.

We shook. "I know. Lark told me your name."

Lark hissed in a breath. "Well, speaking of me, I'm going to go smudge the reception hall." She leaned closer. "Good luck."

Lark hustled away. Mariah called after her. "The caterers just arrived. Don't get in their way."

Lark waved a hand in the air to show she heard, but never turned back.

"Wait! Samantha True?" Mariah said. "I've read all about you in the papers."

I smiled and stuck my hand back in my pocket. "Is there anything you need from me for this wedding? Stella's pretty nervous, and I'd like to make sure it'll go off without a hitch.

Mariah shook her head. "I have it all under control. So you and Leo Stillman, huh?"

You have to respect a person who gets right to it.

"Yep, me and Leo. Speaking of him, I should really see what's keeping him." I whipped out my phone, snapped a picture—albeit not a good one—of Mariah and sent it to him in a text with the words COME NOW following. He wasn't expected at the rehearsal, but now that he was my plus-one and pretend fiancé, his presence wouldn't be out of the ordinary.

He replied: On my way.

Then I shoved my hands and phone back in my pocket.

Mariah glanced at my hands, comfortably tucked in the pockets of my skirt. "Engaged, I heard."

From Leo, since no one in town knew our ruse yet, which meant Mariah and Leo had already seen each other and had a conversation. One where he felt the need to create a fiancée before even asking me to play along. Boy, she must really rattle him because this seemed very out of character for Leo.

"Yeah, engaged." I bit my tongue because I wanted to play it down, as was my nature, but doing so with this woman wouldn't be good. She'd see that as an opening.

"I never saw him as the settling-down type." She clutched her hands to her heart. "I'm sorry, you do know Leo and I have a... past."

I shrugged. "Yeah, you dated in college. I know. I know everything about Leo. I've known him since we were kids."

She smiled, but the insincerity of her smile could be seen in the narrowing of her eyes. "Well, 'dated' doesn't really describe our two years together, but that's all in the past. I sure hope you keep me in mind as a wedding planner."

I gave a thin smile. "Of course."

She wrapped a hand around one long curl. "I suppose Leo has a type." She waved a lock of her hair toward me.

I gave a one-shoulder shrug and looked up at the sky as I thought about the girls Leo dated in high school. "I suppose if, by 'type,' you mean, genuinely nice, family oriented, self-reliant. In high school, Leo dated girls of all hair and skin colors. I think the traits I mentioned were what they had in common." Which made me wonder what he had seen in Mariah if Lark's perception were to be taken into consideration.

A car door slammed in the distance and drew my attention. Mariah glanced in the same direction. Leo was coming toward us. In his hands was my camera bag. He lifted a hand in a one-motion wave.

We watched in silence as he approached us.

"Mariah," he said with a nod. To me, he swung the camera bag up. "Russ said Stella wanted you to grab some photos of today if you could. She forgot to ask you earlier."

I wasn't sure if what he said was true or made up as an excuse for his appearance. He drew closer and cut a sideways glance at Mariah. That's when it dawned on me we needed some public display of affection.

"Great," I said far too loudly. "I'd love to get some photos." I rushed to him and took the bag and wrapped him in a hug at the same time. "Thanks... babe."

In his ear, I whispered. "We're engaged, remember."

He drew me in closer by wrapping an arm around my waist and kissed my temple. "Stella here yet? I saw Tom and Bruce were arriving as I pulled in."

We separated and stood together, his arm still around my waist.

I shook my head. "I haven't seen her."

Mariah looked around the grounds. "The groom is here? In which direction?"

Leo motioned to the reception hall. "They were headed that way."

At that moment, a loud crash of dishes smashing onto the reception hall's tiled floor echoed across the quiet park. Seconds later, Lark stepped out of the building and shouted across the lawn. "Don't worry, the hunky chef and I can totally take care of this mess."

"Dear Lord," Mariah said. "I have to go. As always, I get such pleasure from seeing you, Leo." She hustled off, but not before brushing a hand down his cheek.

Leo stiffened.

I waited until she was out of earshot before I said, "Your ex is... odd. She doesn't seem like someone you'd connect with."

"I could say the same about you and Carson."

"Touché," I said with a laugh. I brushed my hand down the same cheek Mariah had moments ago before following behind her. I needed to find Stella, and I might as well get pictures while I was at it.

"This is going to be fun," I said to him over my shoulder.

He groaned. "I can think of several things more fun. Root canals or being punched in the face. Heck, as much as I hate working homicides, I wouldn't turn one down right now."

3

THURSDAY AFTERNOON

Mariah whipped the catering staff into shape with such precision and authority, it was impressive. And scary.

I'm not ashamed to say I found pleasure in the fact I wasn't the only one with an ex who was better off in the past. Thankfully, mine was dead. Well, I mean, there were times I wondered about that, but truly... Carson was dead. So what if he was a con man with skills up the wazoo. For him to have survived that fiery crash would have taken serious planning and help. And I didn't help him. His best friend, Tyson Lockett, didn't help him. Lockett and I had become close friends, and I think I would have known if he'd helped Carson pull off a stunt like that, all the while lying to me.

Nope. Dead. Carson was dead. And watching Mariah make Leo a nervous mess with her passive-aggressive behavior toward both of us made me appreciate my situation.

I had taken tons of photos of the grounds and Lark smudging the reception hall when I made my way to Leo leaning against a tree outside. If I didn't know better, I might think he was hiding, as his position couldn't be seen from the reception hall.

"What are you doing?" I said, coming up beside him.

He'd been texting on his phone and jumped. "For a second, I thought you were Mariah."

"Why don't you leave? We only really have to be the plus-one tomorrow at the wedding."

He shook his head. "Because I promised Stella I would be here. I want her to know she has my family's support."

And that's when I remembered. Jeez, how could I have forgotten that Stella had once been engaged to Leo's uncle. Maybe because it all happened back when I was still in elementary school. Stella and Leo's Uncle Ben had been in a terrible car accident. Ben had died on impact, leaving Stella to grieve the loss of him and the life they never had. I was embarrassed I'd forgotten, and even more embarrassed for Stella with all this betting talk.

She really did seem to live under a cursed cloud.

"Who do you think I should take for my quarterback in my fantasy team? Hue's telling me to hurry and make my picks.

"Was I invited into this fantasy league? Nope. So why do you think I'd help?" My voice was thick with irritation. My dad was the reigning champ of fantasy football, and because of it, I paid the price. I was never asked to join leagues.

"Crap." Leo turned his phone to face me. "Oliver Gee just texted. The feds have stopped looking into the Austin Strong murder case."

"So, will we ever know who killed him? I mean, how hard is it to get a suspect list? The guy was in jail at the time?"

Leo shrugged. "I'm sorry. At least we know he won't be coming for you, and it's likely Strong being taken out in jail was a paid hit. Strong had a lot of secrets on people."

I gestured with my chin for him to look behind him. "Heads up, incoming."

He glanced over his shoulder and groaned. Bruce Rawlings, the son of Stella's future husband, was making his way toward us. He wore a suit without a tie and kept his dress shirt unbuttoned to the middle of his chest. That he kept one hand in his pants pocket most of the time gave him a smarmy vibe.

"I bet you ten bucks he makes a puke joke," I muttered.

"Not taking it. Because he'll follow it up with a jab at how he trained me or something." He looked at his phone with longing and a second later followed it with a smile. As if an idea popped into his head.

I could almost read his thoughts. I snatched this phone. "Oh no you don't. You aren't leaving me with him. No pretending you're getting a call or something."

Leo glared at me.

"Samantha True! Is it safe to come close? Do you have the flu? No vomiting allowed at my dad's rehearsal dinner or wedding." He put air quotes around the words "the flu."

I pasted on a fake smile. "Ha, ha, Bruce. That was what... ten years ago? And I did have the flu."

He waved two finger-guns at me. "You can keep saying that, Sam, but we all know it was the deer and the scene you couldn't handle. Or maybe it was being around the rookie." He winked at Leo.

Then Bruce thrust out his left hand. "How are ya, Leo. How's the Wind River PD treating you? You know, you tire of working for the public, there's always room for you in the private sector."

Leo and Bruce shook hands.

Leo said, "I heard you'd moved into private security, Bruce. I wasn't aware that you'd gone full time and left the Vancouver PD."

Bruce rocked back on his heels, both hands now in his pockets, and nodded adamantly. "Yeah. Just about a year ago. I'm living the dream, man. No more twenty-four hour workdays, no more paycheck to paycheck."

"Sounds awesome," I said. Leo wouldn't care about that stuff, so I saved him from having to make a fake pleasantry.

Tom, Bruce's dad, and the groom, joined us, a glowing smile on his face. "Samantha. Glad you're standing up with Stella. It means a lot to have people who love her surround her on this special day."

I gave an awkward shrug, as I'm not good with compliments. A side effect of being a misdiagnosed dyslexic. In my early years in school, I was accused of faking it.

I said, "Stella means everything to me. To my family. It's an honor that she asked."

"Who ya bringing to the wedding?" Bruce asked, jabbing my shoulder with his pointer finger. "Anyone special?"

I shifted away from him. "Ah, well. Funny you should ask..." I glanced at Leo, not sure how much I should tell Bruce. I jerked my thumb toward Leo. "I'm going with this guy."

Bruce crossed his arms. "Cool, though I'm surprised, because word around town is that you all have been hanging out, but no action. People are wondering what's going on?"

Leo cleared his throat. "Now they can stop wondering.

Me and Sam. Each other's plus-one. I'm plus-oneing the heck out of this job."

Tom chuckled.

Ugh, this conversation was the worst. But I attempted to blow it off. "You know how it goes, Bruce. My husband's only been dead a year. If I'd hooked up before now, people would've talked, then, too."

Tom sighed and shook his head with sadness. "You're right, Samantha. Outsiders always have a lot to say about the love life of others. You do you, as the kids say."

He squeezed my shoulder in a fatherly way. I thought about what Dad and I talked about. How no one knows about Tom's first wife.

The caterer came up to Tom. "Excuse me, sir. There's a question about the hors d'oeuvres?"

Tom scanned the crowd. "That's better handled by my fiancée. She should be here already, if not any minute. Let me see if I can answer it. Or better yet, her wedding planner can answer it." He walked toward the reception hall with the caterer.

I glanced at my watch. Stella should have arrived by now. "Excuse me a second." As I stepped away, I took my phone out of my pocket. Leo caught my eye, and I gave a slight headshake. He knew I'd tell him in a minute.

I called Dad. He answered on the second ring.

"Sammy, Sam, Sam, what's the good word?" The background noise told me he was driving.

"Dad, have you heard from Stella? She's not at the rehearsal yet."

"Nope, maybe moving that statue thing was more a pain than she thought?" He didn't sound concerned. "It's not like she'd ask for help if it was. Like all the women in my life, she's stubborn."

I snapped my fingers to get Bruce's attention. I didn't want to cause unnecessary worry, but Stella should have been here by now. "What's your address?"

Bruce pointed to himself. "Mine? Why?"

"Because my dad is going to swing by and see if Stella needs help with the statue."

"I can go check on her," Bruce offered.

"I'd rather not have your dad worry. My dad's already in the car. Your address?"

He gave his house number and street. I passed it along to my dad.

"Perfect. We're three minutes away from there."

"Thanks, Daddy-o. Love you."

I went back to Leo and Bruce. Bruce turned his attention to me. "I heard you've given up photography altogether to be a private dick, eh, Sam?"

"No." I nodded to my camera bag that was on the ground next to Leo's feet. "I've been getting pictures for Stella, and I use my camera a lot in my 'private dick' business, as you put it." Yes, I used air quotes. "It's funny you should use that term. You know how the PI business goes. Lots of wandering willies whose wives need proof, and my camera captures lots of those shots."

Leo chuckled.

Bruce waggled his brows. "You're making a name for yourself, that's for sure. Getting AJ Gunn off those murder charges was a lucky break, for sure."

I clenched my hands. "Luck has nothing to do with it. AJ was innocent." And I almost got killed trying to prove it.

Bruce smirked. "Either way, I'll send anyone who's looking for a PI your way."

I almost responded with I'd rather you not but moved the conversation on to other safer topics. Like the Seahawks, and if Bruce was planning any summer trips. We made boring small talk, enough that most people move away to do something less mind-numbing, but not Bruce. He hung out and kept the conversation going.

The ringing of my phone and its matching vibration in my dress pocket caught me off guard.

I pulled it out and looked at the screen, puzzled. This wasn't my phone, but my dad's name was on the screen.

"That's mine, remember," Leo said. He took the phone, quirked a brow when he saw the name, then accepted the call.

He met my gaze and held it.

"Yeah," he said to my dad. "I can be there in under ten. Until then, wait in your car."

I leaned in, trying to hear.

"Yeah, she's right here. I'll tell her." He disconnected the call and looked at Bruce. "Sorry, man. That was Oliver Gee from the station. You remember him? He's having an issue. I need to go. Good seeing you, Bruce." He didn't wait for Bruce to answer any of his questions.

I held my tongue, wondering why he lied about the caller to Bruce.

"Good seeing you too." Bruce said.

Leo took my arm. "I need to talk to Sam a minute. Excuse us." To me, he said. "Walk with me to my car." He bent down and grabbed my camera bag.

We were several steps away before Leo leaned in close and said in a hushed voice, "I don't want Bruce to know this yet. Your dad went to Bruce's house. Stella's not there. But LC is. I need you to follow me to the scene."

"The scene?" I swallowed.

"Your dad says it looks like something bad has happened to her."

THURSDAY AFTERNOON

HAVING AN IMAGINATION IS WONDERFUL. I HAVE A VIVID and active one. Being able to escape from the drudgery of decoding words to someplace else, like space exploration or hunting Big Foot, had been a lifesaver when I was a kid.

But today, right now, my active imagination is coming up with the worst. Leo's use of the word "scene" has brought forth terrible visions of what will be waiting for us when we arrive. Scenes that make me want to pull over and vomit or cry. Or both. I beg the universe that Stella is okay, alive.

I bring Stella's MINI to a screeching halt along the curb across the street from Bruce's house. From where I've parked, I'm able to survey the house and what I'm guessing is what will be the crime scene. It was easy to make out: a shattered statue in pieces across the garage floor. A dark reddish-brown smudge on the garage floor near the bulk of the broken pieces.

There's a numbness that comes with looking at something you know depicts a crime. The feeling is even more difficult to process when the crime was committed against someone you know and love.

LC was backed up in the driveway, the back cargo door open. My mom and dad were standing near their car, holding hands, leaning into each other. Leo went to them.

I slid out of the MINI and rushed to hear what was being said. I followed the path Leo did, trying to maintain the integrity of the crime scene.

My mom folded me in a hug as Dad told his story.

"When we pulled up, it looked just like this. No one around. I called out her name. I went inside the house through the door in the garage and called her name. Nothing."

Mom said, "I tried calling her. I thought maybe she dropped the statue, got cut, and went to a neighbor to get some help or something. But when it started ringing on my end, I heard it also ring in Stella's car. I looked in the window, and her purse and phone were on the seat."

"What was Stella doing here?" Leo asked.

"Picking up a statue that she intended to give to Tom as a wedding gift." I gestured to the debris field. "It was two garden gnomes hugging with a heart between them. She was going to decorate it with white lights."

"There are lights on the seat next to her purse," Mom said.

"Garden gnomes?" Leo asked.

I knew where he was going with this. Tom's landscaping business was known for its classic taste and creative design. Garden gnomes were not and have never been part of the décor. So giving one seemed like the tackiest gift ever.

"Tom and Stella met at the community center. They both signed up to take a French cuisine class. Long story short, the garden gnome was an inside joke for them. I don't know what it means. But the statue was going into their garden at the house. It's a tongue-in-cheek kinda gift."

Leo turned to survey the scene. "Russ, when you say you went inside, how far in did you go?"

Dad shook his head. "Not far. The door opens to a laundry room, and I stepped inside and called Stella's name. I knew she wasn't in there. The house felt empty, know what I mean?"

Both Leo and I nodded. Gut instinct, whatever you want to call it, we'd all honed it through our respective professions and relied upon its accuracy.

"How long would you say from when Stella left the newspaper to when you got here?" Leo asked Dad.

I pulled out my phone and showed Leo the call log. "This is when I called Dad to ask him to swing by. Stella left the office about ten minutes before I did. I stopped at Lark's to ask her to smudge the reception site, and waited while she gathered her stuff. I'd say it's been just over an hour since Stella left the office, around four thirty."

"And we arrived right around five twenty. I know this because I called Cora right before, asking how her spelling test went. She was getting ready for bed," Mom said. Cora was my niece, and ever since Rachel, my sister, had come home from deployment and collected her daughter and returned to Virginia, my mom was having serious Cora with-drawals. But then again, so was I.

Leo was quiet as he continued to stare at the scene.

I said, "If she came directly here, we're looking at a window from quarter to five to five twenty, when she was taken."

"Yep." He moved into the garage and was inspecting

what he could without touching anything. "Sam, can you get your camera?" His gaze met mine.

I gave a brief nod, then jogged off to Stella's MINI. The sound of a deep engine turning over caught my attention. A block down the road, a classic but poorly maintained Bronco eased away from the curb. I pulled out my phone and scrolled through my contacts until I found Toby's number. I pressed call.

"Dudette," he said. "I hope you aren't expecting me to drive, because I'm not driving tonight. There's a John Cusack marathon on TV I want to watch. I got all the comfort foods and a fun Twizzler-flavored vape." To emphasize his words, he made a puffing sound.

"Nope, but I was wondering if you could do some online snooping for me." Toby was my IT guy. I'd inherited him from my dead, and not legally-wedded husband. One of the best things I'd ever gotten from Carson.

"That I can do. *Hot Tub Time Machine* is on. I've seen this, like, one hundred times." He crunched on something.

"What are you eating?" I was used to the Doritos crunch. This was different.

"Takis. Spicy. And in case you were wondering, this is how I like to add spice to my life, Sam. Not by being chased or shot at or anything like that."

"Then anytime we do a road trip, you should stay home." Road trips seemed to be when the bad stuff happened. "Toby, Stella's missing. Someone nabbed her from Bruce Rawlings' house."

"Crap on a cracker. Not Stella. Someone is gonna seriously get some bad karma. Okay, so I'm guessing you want me to shop the information sites and look into the groom, Tom, right? I mean, we all wonder about his past. Dude just showed up and was part of the community. Always so nice and helpful. If he did this, then I am for sure going on the road trip to chase him down into the ground."

I snickered. "Okay, noted. But first, let's make sure he had a reason to do this. I don't want to waste precious time chasing down the wrong leads."

From behind me, the return of the deep, rumbling engine caught my attention. The sound was something I was familiar with. It was similar to the one LC made, and it spoke about the age and mechanical needs of the engine.

I glanced behind me to see the same Bronco that had pulled away from the curb minutes earlier, crossing down the street. Likely answer was rubberneckers, curious about what might be going on. But I would not hedge my bets there. Tucking the phone between my ear and shoulder, I snatched up my camera and readied it to grab some shots. I aimed my camera in their direction and pressed the shutter button, holding it down to get several sequential shots.

The driver of the Bronco must have caught sight of me, because the vehicle sped up. I managed a few shots of the license plate before it sped away.

"Hey, can you also look up this license plate?" I flipped through the digital screen until I found an excellent shot and enlarged it. I read the plate digits off.

"Consider it done. I'll call you ASAP." *Crunch crunch.*

"Thanks." I disconnected and grabbed my messenger bag from the front seat. I then put the bag on, tucking my phone into the side pocket. I surveyed the street again, looking for the Bronco or anything else. A dark high-end electric sedan was parked along the curb six houses behind me. That a person was sitting in the driver's seat watching us was what caught my attention.

The driver wore a ball cap. Again, it could be nothing. But I raised my camera and zoomed in to get a few shots. The windows were tinted, and coupled with the ball cap, the images were poor. The driver looked in my direction. The skin on my neck crawled. Then, without any engine sound, he whipped the car into a three-point turn and sped off. I snagged a few shots of the license and texted them to Toby as well.

I jogged back to where Leo was standing in the garage. He's asked my parents to wait by their car. My dad, an investigative reporter by trade, was already assessing the situation. He knew Leo had found something. He also knew I'd fill him in later, but that didn't stop him from watching anyway, so he could later compare my notes with what he observed.

I glanced back down the road, first in one direction, then the other. I turned to find Leo giving me a puzzled look.

I explained my actions. "There was a Bronco that was parked along the curb, then drove by. And a Tesla parked down the road as well. Likely nothing, but I'm having Toby check their plates. I'm also having Toby look into Tom. He's the first suspect, right?"

"Sadly, yes. Oliver Gee is already on his way to the reception hall to question Tom. I expect they'll show up here soon. So let's get these pics before they get here." He pointed to an impression in the unpainted drywall of the garage. The wall was indented with a smudge of makeup. I adjusted my lens and snapped shots from various angles. Leo held up a quarter next to the impression to get the size shot.

On his notepad he wrote that shot one was the impression in the wall. He indicated to a second impression. This was a large scrape where some wall had been gouged out. The gouge was the width of my three fingers and the length of my forearm. We got a series of shots, including the size shot. Leo marked this down as number two. He then labeled the trail of small, brownish-red drops on the ground that led to the smear and to where the statue had dropped and shattered into its current state of a million pieces.

More blood, but still a small amount. I photographed them.

I was squatting to get shots by the floor when I looked up at Leo. "This is what I'm thinking." I motioned to the first spot we logged. "Stella was here, bent over to pick up the statue, when someone grabbed her. She fell forward or was pushed forward, her head hitting the wall."

"Yeah, and either her head got cut from that impact or it was her hand." He tapped his pen on spot two.

"They grabbed her, she fell forward, and they lifted her up. Knowing Stella, she put up a fight."

"All while holding the statue."

"Which wasn't small, and it had to have been heavy. They swung her around, and I'm guessing the tips of the gnomes' hats made that groove."

"Which is where she could have scraped her head, making it bleed."

I pointed to spot three. "This is where they got control of her and she dropped the statue. A lack of significant blood makes me think her injuries aren't life threatening and that she's still alive."

Leo gave me a small smile. "Yeah, silver lining. I'd agree with your summarization."

I'm the type of person who has to say the bad things. If I keep them in my head, they can become overwhelming. I said, "Because if they wanted to kill Stella, she would be dead, and they would have left her body behind."

"Sure."

"Sure" is Leo's way of not committing.

I added, "In most cases, right?"

He met my gaze. "Yes, in most cases."

I looked out at the driveway, my parents, and LC.

"Who would want to kidnap Stella and why? Or is she just a pawn in a game where we have no idea who the players are?"

"But we will know. There's no question about that." Leo set his jaw in determination.

Anger coursed through me. Because my family was so close to Stella, I couldn't help but take this personally. Little else made me angrier than someone going after the people I love.

"And when we do learn, I'm gonna use my stun gun on them several times, and I'm gonna enjoy every zap."

5

THURSDAY AFTERNOON

I ADDED SHOTS OF LC AND THE INTERIOR, INCLUDING the open cargo space. My car keys were still in the ignition. A clue that she hadn't planned on staying long.

Leo stood beside me. "You know, there's one thing you haven't mentioned."

I looked at him, puzzled. "About all this?"

He nodded. "Yes, a second possibility."

I glanced around, trying to figure out what I missed. I looked back at Leo and he motioned at LC.

"Maybe whoever did this was here because they thought it was you?"

I gulped. "Maybe the last wish of Austin Strong?"

Making enemies was something that came with the territory of being a PI. I just never really thought I'd make an enemy who would want to kill me. Naïve, I know.

Leo put his hand up. "It's an alternate theory. Let's just work the case and see where it takes us."

"Don't say anything to my parents."

He gave me a look that indicated he thought I was crazy. "Why would you even think I'd do that?"

"Because I'm freakin' out. It's bad enough that Stella is missing, but maybe missing because they mistook her for me. Ugh, I can't even..."

"Work the case. What do you want to do next?"

Thinking about what was next was the perfect distraction. "I'm going to see if any of the neighbors have a door camera."

But before we could continue our conversation, a silver Land Rover Discovery sped up to the driveway and came to a screeching halt inches from Leo's pickup truck. A cop car was behind the Rover. Oliver Gee jumped out of the patrol car and rushed toward the Rover. He shot Leo a look of dismay.

Tom Rawlings stumbled out of the passenger side of the Rover and staggered up the drive, his hands in his hair. "Oh my God, oh my God, please tell me she's not dead."

Leo put up his hands and hurried to keep Tom from entering any further into the crime scene. "Mr. Rawlings, calm down. We have no reason to believe that Stella isn't alive."

Bruce ran from the driver's side of the Rover to his dad. "Pop, calm down. You have to get a grip." He glanced at Leo. "Leo is one of the best cops I know. I promise you, he's already five steps ahead of us. But you need to calm down."

Tom spun on Bruce. He grabbed him by the front of his shirt, his fist buried deep. "I can't go through something like this again. I can't lose Stella. It's not right or fair." His voice wobbled, and my interest, though already piqued, was now heightened. What did he mean he couldn't go through this again? How many times had he gone through this before? How many former Mrs. Toms were out there and were they all still alive?

"Pop, it's going to be okay. I promise."

"You can't promise that."

Bruce eased his dad's hands from his shirt. "We'll get through his together. But first let's find out what happened." He squeezed his dad's hands and drew him in for a hug.

Tom pulled away and turned his attention back to Leo. "Tell me what happened. Was she mugged? Did she come upon someone trying to rob Bruce's house?"

Leo nodded at Bruce. "I'm going to need you to do a walk-through with me to see if you were burgled."

Bruce rubbed a hand down his face. "Okay."

To Tom, Leo said, "Mr. Rawlings, it would seem that Stella was abducted. We already have some leads."

Bruce straightened. "You do? That's outstanding. I want to offer my services. I'm going to put a few men on Dad to make sure he's protected. If Stella was taken, I don't want Dad to be next."

"Assuming this was planned and not a crime of opportunity," Leo said.

Bruce replied, "Yeah. Assuming."

My phone, tucked in my bag, vibrated. I stepped away to take the call.

"What do you have for me, Toby?"

His response was a slurping sound. "Sorry, just finishing my Slurpee. I had To-The-Door dropped a few minutes ago." To-The-Door was a food delivery service.

"Awesome, what's up?"

He cleared his throat. "So I had to do some digging to get

some background on Tom. In fact, I'm still scraping together info to make sure I didn't miss anything. I didn't know where to start, so I pulled up Bruce's Wind River police force résumé and started with where he went to high school and such. That's where I got lucky."

I know Toby couldn't see me, but I waved for him to get to the point. I also knew saying as much would only lead to more of a delay in getting the information I wanted. To a degree, Toby needed to toot his own horn.

"Where did Bruce go to high school?"

"Eastern Washington. Near Spokane. That's where he joined the force. They relocated here a few years later."

"Because?" I dug deep for patience.

"Well, there's no website or blog to say why. But my best guess is because Tom's wife and youngest child, his daughter, were killed in a car accident. A year later, they moved here. Bruce joined Wind River, where he served for twelve years before moving on to Vancouver to become a detective."

I glanced at Tom. Is that what he meant about not being able to do this again? He meant losing someone, not that he couldn't go through another abduction.

"Tom never remarried after his wife died?"

"Nope." *Crunch crunch.* "Not that I can find. Until our amazing Stella came along."

In a flash, I went from scrutinizing everything Tom said and did because I saw him as a suspect, to wanting to hug him because now he was a victim, like me. Someone he loved, someone he wanted to spend his life with was suddenly gone, and none of his life made any sense at this moment.

"Okay. Thanks, Toby. That's helpful."

"Yeah, I kinda feel like a douche. He was my suspect numero uno until, like, one minute ago when I finished reading the article. I'll send it to you. It's a sad article."

"Okay, anything else?" I didn't want to assume that he'd gotten all my requests done, but it would be odd if he hadn't.

"I'm hitting a wall with the second car tag. The car belongs to a shell company, and so I'm doing some back tracing. I should have something soon. But the Bronco belongs to a two-bit criminal with a rap sheet of petty crime, including burglary and robbery. His name is Leslie Stone. Goes by Les, has a sidekick who's known on the street as Sticks. Real name, Rick Richards. Rap sheet looks similar. Mug shot shows two enormous doofuses."

"How do you mean?"

"I look at these two, and I see the idiots from that *Home Alone* movie. Wanna guess what Leslie's street name is?"

"I can't even begin," I said.

"Stone. They call themselves Sticks and Stone. Morons." *Crunch crunch.* "But I'm gonna laugh about it all night, because why not."

"Why not indeed. Thanks, Toby. And let me know when you get the other plate info."

"Will do, Sam the man."

"What?"

"I dunno. I'm kinda wanting a street name now too. I think we should all have them."

I chuckled. It was high time; what did I expect? "Well, you give it some thought. I'll be here if you come up with something better than Sam the man,"

"Roger that, Captain."

"By chance, are you watching *Pirates of the Caribbean?*"

"Aye." He slurped more of his drink. "I switched from my Cusack marathon to this."

I laughed some more and disconnected. I made my way to Leo. He'd gotten Tom to sit inside the Rover while Bruce was inside doing a walk-through with Officer Gee.

Leo met me halfway and I leaned close, wanting to keep our conversation private. I told him about what Toby found out about Tom's past.

"You got any info on the two characters, Sticks and Stone? I want to see if I can chase them down."

"Let's do that together. They may be petty, but word is they're trying to level up." He motioned toward the house. "This might be a way to do it."

"You think they were casing the neighborhood and saw Stella and jumped at the opportunity?"

He shrugged.

"That means they know who she is."

"Maybe, or they think she's you. Or maybe they knew this was Bruce's house. Maybe they saw something and wanted to level up that way. Really, we have lots of possibilities. Let's not make assumptions."

"Leo, Leo, look, I got this text," Tom hollered from the Rover. He jumped out, waving his phone, and rushed toward Leo.

Leo glanced at the screen, then showed it to me. The message said: 3 Million for the lady. You have 24 hours. More to follow. No cops.

He asked Tom, "Do you recognize this number?"

Tom shook his head.

I snort-laughed. "They're stupid. No cops. They took her from a cop's house."

Tom shook his head. "Well, he's not really with the department anymore. Doing his own private business."

I didn't want to argue that Bruce was still a cop at heart. He still had connections. Logic is hard when so many emotions are ruling.

"I have to call the bank. I have to move money around."

"We should bring in the FBI," Leo advised.

"No." Tom shook his head adamantly. "They said no cops."

"They always say that," I added. Not that I knew this from real life, but didn't every TV show or movie have this in it? "Right?"

Leo nodded. "Let's not make any hasty decisions. Let me see if I can get a location by tracing this number. Let me follow up on those leads we have. There are lots of steps we need to do before we rush to hand over three million dollars."

Leo's tone was soothing and calm. I was ready to comply even though I knew the number was likely from a burner phone and that lead would go nowhere.

Tom, on the other hand, wanted to comply with the wrong people. "You're right. There are lots of steps. First, I need to call Pete. He's the president of my bank. I'll need him to open up the bank so I can make a withdrawal."

At that moment, Bruce came out of the house. Tom caught sight of him and rushed to his son. "I got a ransom demand. Three million. I need you to take me to Pete's house, now."

Leo turned to me. "I need you to find Sticks and Stone. Call me at first sighting. They like to hang out near downtown. Pawnshops are where they are often found."

"Because they're always fencing stolen goods?"

"Yeah. Drive around and hopefully you'll see Stone's Bronco. Call me if you do. We'll tag-team them."

Oliver joined us. "Nothing missing from the house that he can tell."

Leo said to Oliver, "Go try to talk Tom off the ledge. But please don't mention bodies or anything gruesome. When you get him settled, start knocking on doors and see who has cameras facing this direction."

Oliver sucked in a breath, then headed over to where Bruce was attempting to calm his father down.

"When can I get LC back?"

Leo shrugged. "In a few days, probably. We're going to have to process LC and pull prints. Can't assume whoever did this didn't go into your SUV."

I groaned.

Leo pulled something from his pocket and returned his attention to me. "Listen, I wanted to give you this, but I didn't know how."

He held out a Seahawks key chain with a fat medallion hanging from a silver chain.

"It's not just a key chain. It's a tracker. It's also an SOS button. Something goes south, you press the medallion, and I get a text alerting me. The app gives me your location."

I opened my mouth to... Protest? Say thanks? I wasn't sure how I felt about a tracker.

He pointed to my face. "That! That right there is why I hesitated." He dropped his hand and sighed. "I'm not trying to track you, Sam. But what if this had been about you?" He nodded to the crime scene. "And truthfully, after getting some scary phone calls from you, like the time you were assaulted or the time you were hit by the car, I worry that there will be a time when you won't have your phone, or it won't work, and you won't be able to reach me or anyone."

"Leo."

"I don't want anything to happen to you. And I know this feels invasive. But think about it. Think of it as a backup plan. You can clip the chain off and stick it in your little pouch." He gently touched my waist.

He looked to be almost pleading. And he was right. The medallion would fit perfectly in the little pouch I made and pinned inside my waistband. The tools inside were tools I've learned I needed to have on hand. The pocketknife had actually saved my life.

"Okay," I said. "I'll think about it. I'll carry it around for a while and consider it."

"That's all I can ask for. It was Hue's idea, by the way."

I adjusted the messenger bag on my shoulder, slipping the medallion in the front pocket. "You know, you don't have to sell it to me through Hue. I don't like it more because he might have suggested it. I trust you, Leo. I know you have my best interest at heart. And I'm thankful for that." I squeezed his forearm.

He stared into my eyes. Trying to read me, maybe? I stared back. Something I can't define passed between us. All this energy and feelings between us were relatively new. I'd spent the better portion of my life being ignored by Leo, so whatever this was we were experiencing was refreshing and weird at the same time. And I won't lie, my girly parts were excited by it.

I thought for a second he might kiss me. I thought for another second I might kiss him. The tension between us cracked and made me uncomfortable, so I leaned in and whispered, "Besides, we're engaged. This feels very much like something a fiancé would do."

He grinned and brushed a hand down my cheek.

"I'll call you if I come across Sticks and Stone." My voice sounded husky and raw.

"No going rogue, we're a team."

"A team," I echoed before stepping away. I liked how that sounded.

6

THURSDAY AFTERNOON

I WAITED UNTIL I WAS AROUND THE CORNER FROM Bruce's house before I pulled to the curb and turned the SOS button over and over in my hand. Panic button, tracker, whatever you wanted to call it. This little doohickey represented two things to me.

One, that I lived a life that required an emergency plan should an attack happen. And the likelihood of one happening was good since they'd already happened in the past. And two, that Leo and I were in a different place. Our past was not a happy or a friendly one. Yet there was no denying that Leo has been my guardian angel since everything went sideways with Carson.

I stared down at the little button. Had Carson given me this, I would have been suspicious. I would have felt like he was tracking me under the guise of safety. But Leo? Nah, I saw how distressed he was when he brought it up.

I texted Hue. I started with a button emoji: SOS. How long?

Hue and I liked to communicate in symbols. Maybe

because we were both dyslexic, and pictures were easier. Or maybe now it was just fun to stump one another.

Hue's text included praying hands and a person bowing: *Finally!* 1 mo.

Hue's symbols were his version of thank the Lord.

A month?

My phone rang. Hue.

"What? An actual call? Usually you're too busy," I said instead of the standard hello.

"Can you believe it? The clocks lined up. What are you doing right now, that my brother finally gave you the SOS button?"

"Stella's been kidnapped. Like just within the last hour." I tried not to cry.

Hue groaned. "No wonder he gave it to you. Be careful, Sam. Something I've perfected in the marines is to compartmentalize. Get emotional when you find her. Not before then."

I nodded even though he couldn't see me. "Yeah, I've been telling myself that. I have a powerful urge to ram LC into cars or buildings belonging to the people I suspect and to ask questions later."

"Lock it down."

"Oh, shut up." Hue liked to talk to me like I was one of his brothers-in-arms. Which, in a weird way, I was. "A month, huh? He said it was your idea."

Hue chuckled. "Maybe, kinda. He said he was worried and wished he could attach one of those Life Alert buttons to you. I told him about this. Giving this to you was hard for him. He's not one to invade another's privacy. But you're giving him heartburn."

I smiled. "I could tell it wasn't easy. It's just weird, ya

know. Getting close to Leo. It's familiar because of you, I suppose, and different."

Hue dropped his voice and said seductively, "How close are you two getting?"

"Go pound sand."

"Seriously, though. Back in high school he asked me once if I had it bad for you."

"Gross," I teased.

"Yeah, I said the same thing. I don't think he believed me. Because he asked me again last year. I can't help but wonder..."

"What?"

"Nothing, time will tell."

"Are you saying you think Leo—"

"I'm saying I think you should let things play out and not talk yourself out of something because you're scared."

"Scared of what? I mean, besides the usual spider, horror movies, special sauces on burgers with chunks in them."

"I'm saying you're afraid to take chances on people. Romantic chances."

"Ugh, Hue, I took a chance, and look where it got me." A dead husband who I wasn't legally married to.

"You only took that chance because you were in Vegas, had too much to drink, and your mom had been riding you about relationships and such. You would have never married Carson otherwise, and I would put money on that."

"You're saying I avoid romantic involvement?"

"Like the plague."

"So do you." I was being petulant.

"Totally. We're both a mess. But we both deserve happiness, don't we?"

"Yeah, we do." I stared at the button. I leaned back in my seat and tucked the small piece in my secret pocket. "I'll go get some if you do."

"Deal."

"I miss you, Hue. Come home for a visit sooner than later, okay?"

"That's the plan. Be careful out there. Trust your gut. Don't let your emotions get the best of you, and watch your six."

"I can say the same to you, you know." He had a deployment coming up.

We disconnected. I needed this call to Hue like I need coffee in the morning. With Stella being kidnapped, with my confusion about Leo, my emotions were running high and really taking control of me.

Hue was right. I needed to compartmentalize. There would be time soon enough for me to figure out this cluster of feelings I have for Leo. Right now, I needed to figure out who grabbed Stella.

I texted Precious, telling her we had a case and to call me when she was done for the day. I knew she had an important client meeting, so I didn't expect a quick reply.

I texted Toby. Any ideas on where I can find Sticks and Stone?

Toby: Sticks likes to post on Facebook where he is. Not the sharpest tool. They like Krispy Kreme in Hazel Dell or Chick-fil-A by the mall.

Me: Thanks.

I sent Leo a voice text. "Driving by Krispy Kreme and Chick Fil-A to scout for Sticks and Stone. Any other suggestions?"

He sent me a thumbs-up and a guy doing a shoulder shrug. I assumed he didn't have any other suggestions. Could be that he was busy when I texted.

I put Stella's MINI into drive but didn't get away from the curb before my phone rang. It was my dad.

"Where are you?" I asked, wondering if Leo had cut them free.

"We're headed to the rehearsal dinner to tell people to go home. Then we're heading back home. Well, Mom is. I'm going back to the newspaper. I want you to keep me informed every step of the way." I could tell I was on speaker as my dad's voice sounded farther from the phone than was typical.

"We're really worried about Stella, Sam," Mom said. "I don't like this ransom. I don't trust they'll let her go. Whoever these maniacs are."

"That's why I want to get ahead of this if I can. I want to find her before the clock is up."

"Be careful," they said in unison. "Don't go alone."

"Leo made me promise the same. We're doing this together." This would make them both feel relatively better, though my dad was likely the first to be skeptical.

"What can I do to help, Sammy?" Dad asked.

"Take a picture of who is left at the rehearsal for me, please. And can you make a list of the relatives from Stella's previous husbands? Anyone local that I can drop in on that I might not think of. I know she had two stepdaughters with Jeff." Jeff had been her last husband.

"Done," he said. "I'll text you soon."

"Love you, guys." I disconnected the call.

I pulled away from the curb and decided Hazel Dell Krispy Kreme would be the first place I would drive by.

Time to make a plan.

Compartmentalize. First, create a suspect list. Second, go pound the pavement, and talk to anyone and everyone. Third, trust no one will be telling the truth. And finally, waste no more time.

7

THURSDAY AFTERNOON

I DROVE BY KRISPY KREME THREE TIMES. WENT through the drive-through only once, which showed remarkable restraint if I did say so myself. After the sugar rush from the donut, I circled Chick-fil-A like a shark and hoped to see their Bronco and maybe score a sandwich. Evening had set in, and I hoped perhaps Sticks and Stone would decide to go out for dinner. By not crossing paths with them, didn't it mean they had Stella and were holed up somewhere?

The mall parking lot surrounding the chicken fast-food restaurant was hopping. The fact that Five Guys Burgers was next to the chicken shop didn't help. Cars were everywhere.

I pulled Stella's MINI—who I named Winnie because it rhymed—into a spot where I could watch all the comings and goings, and idled. Yeah, hoping that Sticks and Stone were predictable enough that one of these two spots would produce them was probably an exercise in futility.

I voice-texted Toby: Home address for these yahoos?

He texted back both addresses. I was surprised to find they were a short drive away.

I called Leo before heading out.

"How's it going?"

"Almost done here," he said. "Where are you?"

"I'm driving around Sticks and Stone's favorite food joints, but thinking of doing a drive by one or both of their homes."

"No, wait for me. Because if they're home, we can knock on the door. Any good food where you are?"

I told him about the Chick-fil-A and the Five Guys Burgers next door.

"I'm starving. Can you grab me a burger and some fries? I'm leaving now and will meet you there. We can come up with a game plan together."

The thought of food made me smile. "Yeah, easy-peasy."

We ended the call, and I went into the burger place, though I planned on getting a shake from the chicken shop.

Getting our orders took the better part of fifteen minutes. I was back in Winnie eating fries from the bag and working on an Oreo cookie milkshake when a beat-up, old Bronco caught my eye. The vehicle was circling the drive-through, likely assessing the line and how fast it was moving. I leaned forward, trying to identify the driver. I mean, I was fairly confident it was them because what are the odds someone else has a crappy Bronco like theirs? But one never knows, so I looked through the windshield, straining to make out the driver.

The Bronco pulled up a curb away from the drive-through and traffic route. Sticks jumped out and beat feet into the Chick-fil-A. I tossed a handful of fries in my mouth and stuck my milkshake between my legs. Then I prepped

Winnie for a chase, my goal to follow them. Having been inside to get my shake, I knew the line moved faster than the drive-through, so I wanted to be ready with no notice.

A few minutes later, Sticks ran out with three bags and a drink carrier. With three drinks.

Three? From where I sat, there looked to be only two in the SUV. Sure, they could take the drink and food to someone else. That's plausible.

But what if they had Stella tied up on the floor in the cargo space of the Bronco? What if the extra stuff was for her?

My mind raced with the possibilities. What if they truly had Stella? What if grabbing her had been a crime of opportunity, and now they were like, WTF? Ugh, I didn't really like the thought of them not being prepared and possibly panicky. What if they were hired to grab her and were going to drop her off somewhere? What if these guys didn't have her because they already dropped her off.

Regardless of what scenario was true, I felt Leo and I could take these guys.

Sticks jumped into the Bronco, and they took off with me following behind. I tried to keep my distance, to not be right on their tail. But the stream of cars I'd put between us as we exited the mall all turned off to get onto the interstate, while the Bronco went straight.

I stayed two car lengths behind, sipping on my milkshake as we drove. Their path comprised of riding slowly by various strip malls. They stopped to talk to one dude walking down the street from Dairy Queen, which forced me to drive past them, then pull into a convenience store parking lot to turn around. They looked to be driving around aimlessly.

And Sticks never left the passenger seat. I'd hoped he'd

climb in the back and feed Stella, giving me the proof I needed.

Maybe this was how they "tortured" her. Eating food she couldn't have and going nowhere. The unknowing would drive me wild and Stella too. She was a planner.

They headed toward the river, and for a second I panicked, wondering why they were headed in that direction. Too many true crime stories of dead people in bodies of water, I supposed. Then I remembered Sticks's house was by the river. From what I recalled of the address, his home was about ten miles from where we were.

My phone rang, and I put it on speaker.

"Where are you?" Leo asked. "I'm in the parking lot and I don't see you."

Whoops.

"I saw Sticks and Stone. They got food and I'm following them. They had three drinks in their drink carrier and three bags of food, and there are only two people in the car."

"Sam."

"I'm just tailing them to see what they do. I won't talk to them or anything without you."

"You think they have Stella, but two of those drinks could be shakes, and one could be water or something."

I hated he had a point. The thought of Stella out of reach was wearing on me.

"It's just a harmless tail to see if they do anything noteworthy."

The Bronco braked and slowed down considerably, forcing me to do the same. I looked ahead and couldn't see any reason for the change in their speed. Inside the Bronco, Sticks had turned around and was looking out the back window. At me.

"I've been made," I said more to myself but also to Leo.

The Bronco jerked in sudden acceleration and sped off. Part reflex, part because of my competitive nature, I slammed down on the gas, shifted into a higher gear, and barreled after them.

"Sam, please tell me you aren't chasing them."

I closed in on their back end, and when Sticks turned to look at me, I waved. "Chasing? Nah. They're driving around, and I want to know where they're going."

They changed lanes and so did I, keeping Winnie with enough distance between us that should they suddenly brake, I'd be able to stop without colliding with them. I wasn't a fool all the time. Just occasionally.

We played a game of speed up and slow down for about a mile. All while Leo was scolding me.

"What's the purpose of this, Sam? Just back off, and we can regroup. We'll find them again. They aren't going anywhere."

"I know that. I just have this sense of urgency. That we need to talk to them. What if she's in there?"

Leo groaned. "It's not likely."

"But that's not a one hundred percent guarantee. And we all know life is stranger than fiction. The scenarios of what could be truly happening are numerous."

The Bronco got over into the far right lane. I did the same. We had turned away from the river and were heading back toward the mall.

Sticks stuck his head out of the Bronco. The vehicle suddenly braked; I did the same. Sticks tossed a cup in my direction. It caught some wind and smashed into my windshield, coating the passenger side with a milkshake. From the dark chunks on my windshield, I guessed it was another Oreo shake. What a waste.

"What was that?"

I grimaced. "He threw a shake at my car."

"Just stop, Sam. Please."

I sighed. "Leo, I'm in traffic. I can't just stop. But I will. I promise." I wanted a few more seconds. Up ahead was the on ramp to 205 East. If I were a betting girl, I would guess Sticks and Stone were going to get on the interstate and head east. East was where Stone lived. I prepared to swerve right onto the ramp to follow them. The Bronco braked. I slammed on mine to keep the distance between us. The food bags tipped off the passenger seat, spilling Leo's burger onto the floorboards. Oddly, the fries container was empty.

Then with no warning, the Bronco jerked to the left, crossed four lanes of traffic, jumped a curb on the driver's side, and cut off other cars as they headed for the on-ramp to go west on 205.

I stared stunned at the Bronco, cursing my luck at not being able to follow without causing a major accident. From the back seat on the driver's side, Sticks's pasty-white ass was hanging out of the open window. His moon displayed for all the other drivers to see.

"Crap," I said.

"What?" Leo shouted.

I'd forgotten he was there.

"They ditched me. And they mooned me."

Leo chuckled.

"It's not funny."

He sucked in a heavy breath. "You're right. It's not. But it could be worse. You could have been in an accident. Now come to Chick-fil-A and give me my food."

"About that, I may have unknowingly eaten all your fries."

"Of course you did. It's gonna be okay, Sam. We'll find Stella."

His words were an attempt to console me, but I wasn't feeling it. I was feeling frustration. In fact, I wished I had rear-ended the Bronco because then I could rest, knowing Stella wasn't in the SUV with Sticks and his white ass with the giant, egg-shaped, red birthmark.

8

THURSDAY AFTERNOON

Leo was idling in his patrol car in the parking lot of the mall. I pulled beside him and made it so our driver's-side windows aligned.

I handed him the bag with his burger. "I drank your shake on the way over here. Sorry. I was distressed."

He held up a cup, the whipped cream on the shake still sitting on top. "I figured. I got one when I got fries."

I rested my forehead on the steering wheel, watching Leo from the corner of my eye. "What if Stella was in that Bronco?"

Leo paused while unwrapping his burger. "I just heard from Oliver Gee. He said the house across the street and one down had a door camera. We got the video. I haven't seen it yet, but he said there were two men in the video. The video picks up the front end of Stone's Bronco. Seconds later, Sticks comes into view walking toward Bruce's house. From the opposite side, a guy with a ball cap runs toward the house, stops short, turns, and then runs back from where he came. Moments later, a black Tesla flies past the house. Seconds after that, the Bronco peels away too."

"They didn't take Stella?"

Leo shrugged as he took a bite. He gestured for me to continue with my thoughts.

"Who was the second guy?"

"Dunno yet, wearing a ball cap pulled low, Oliver said. He's going to send me the video."

"That lines up with the pictures I took of the guy in the Tesla." I paused to organize my thoughts. "Okay, so just because they didn't put her in their car doesn't mean they didn't take her. They could have worked with someone else who took her. Makes me think this wasn't a crime of opportunity. Which then makes me wonder who all knew that Stella was going to Bruce's house and used that as an opportunity to snatch her? Few people could have known. Me, Dad, Dan, Bruce, Lark, maybe Mariah."

"Or they could have been following her."

"Doesn't the fact that they have asked for a ransom mean they knew they weren't kidnapping me. Everyone knows my family doesn't have three million. But people know Tom is loaded. His frequent large donations to various organizations in the community tell me that. I mean when he landed the landscaping contract for the new waterfront project, the paper—my dad's paper—told anyone reading how much the contract was for."

He shrugged. "Do you remember how much?"

I shook my head while I pulled out my phone. I did a quick search for the article. I found the information and stared at Leo, eyes wide. "Three million."

"Okay, I'll look into who else was bidding for that and

lost out. We have to unravel this, one strand at a time." His phone chimed, and he glanced at the screen.

I knew something had changed by how he calmly set his burger down but also how his lips thinned. "Looks like Tom got another text message. They want the drop to happen in ten hours."

"Did they say where?"

"Where the reception is being held."

Ten hours from now was six in the morning. The wildlife refuge, the location for the reception, would be quiet and isolated. There wasn't any surrounding housing. The people who ran the place didn't live on-site. "How do they expect to collect the money at such an isolated site?"

"I don't think they do. I think it will change at the last minute to keep us hopping."

"Why do you think they moved up the drop time?"

"Who knows? It could be something as stupid as they have another appointment."

A horrific thought crossed my mind. "Or my actions with Sticks and Stone could have spurred them on. I could have caused this."

He shook his head. "Don't go there, Sam. That's not likely."

"But possible."

"*Anything* is possible." He glanced at his phone and groaned.

"What?"

He pressed two fingers to his temple. "They want *you* to make the drop."

"What? Me? Why me?"

He shook his head. "I don't like it."

"What if I caused all of this?" I banged my hand against the steering wheel.

"Sam, stop. That's not productive. You didn't ask anyone to kidnap Stella. You aren't to blame."

I appreciated he didn't sugarcoat or try to make me feel better. Yeah, his words didn't alleviate any guilt, but his words kept me focused. Finding Stella was the goal. Spinning my wheels, feeling sorry for myself wasn't going to get that done.

"I have to head back to the station. Oliver is trying to talk Tom off the ledge. Bruce wants to send some of his security guys to stake out the place and set up cameras. Talking to Sticks and Stone will have to wait a bit. DB is out of town, so the station is short staffed." DB was the police chief and the greatest idiot to walk the planet. I should know; he tried to cheat off me in chemistry. Me, the dyslexic.

"Okay, I'm going to touch base with Toby. I'll let you know my plans after that."

He gave me a thumbs-up. "Want the rest of my shake?"

I shook my head. "I think I should stop at two."

He chuckled. "At some point, I'll want you to walk through Stella's house. See if anything stands out."

"Has anyone told Stella's stepdaughters—former step-daughters—she's missing?"

"No. Because they aren't related anymore, technically."

I shook my head. "I'll do it. She's still close to them."

"Sounds like a plan." He winked, then drove away.

I put my call to Toby on speaker. He answered on the second ring.

"Dudette!"

"Can you get me Jessica MacInerney's address? I need to tell her about Stella."

"I'm way ahead of you. I was scouring social media to see if there had been any leak about Stella, and... jeez... forget high time, this shit is shocking."

"What's shocking?"

"The absolute rage Jessica MacInerney-Jones feels for Stella."

Jessica was one of Stella's stepdaughters. Or I suppose that's how she could be defined so long as Stella was her dad's widow. Would that still be the case once Stella remarried?

Jessica and Stella had always been close, so what Toby was saying was shocking.

"Hate? What? How?"

He belched. "Sorry, carbonated drinks do that to me. I don't know how or why, but Jessica's social media is riddled with calling Stella names, even alludes to her possibly being a black widow, killing off her husbands when she tires of them."

I gasped. I knew Jessica, albeit not very well. If I saw her out and about, we'd stop and exchange pleasantries, but we weren't on each other's contact list or anything. We hadn't grown up together or in the same town. We'd been out of high school when Stella married Jessica's dad, Oscar.

"I'm stunned," I said.

"Yeah, well, I did some digging, and you know how Jessica started her own cake-baking company."

"Yeah?"

"She's in over her head debtwise. From what I can tell, she hasn't made a cake in six months."

"How long has she had financial problems?" Stella had inherited a lot when Oscar passed away.

"A few months after Oscar died, the cakes stopped being

made. As I see it, she stopped baking, and debt started rolling in."

"How long since the ugly post about Stella started?"

"Around the same time. Just know I'm splicing this together with Facebook posts and other crap."

"So you could be misreading this?"

"Not a chance."

I sighed. "I'm gonna head over to Jessica's. Leo says they haven't told the MacInerney's about Stella being taken. I guess I'll be that bearer of bad news. I'll see how she reacts. Do you have her address?"

"Yep, East Vancouver. Be careful, Sam." He gave me Jessica's physical address.

"Always."

He cleared his throat.

"Is there something you're not telling me?"

There was a pause while he took a sip of something. His gulps came in quick successions.

"Toby?"

Lady M, Toby's emotional support animal, cooed.

"You're freaking me out, Toby."

"All right, she maybe made one or two negative posts about you."

"What? Seriously?"

"Yeah."

"How many posts? One or two?"

"Four."

I've lost the capacity for words. "About me?"

"Yeah."

"What do they say?"

"One is a link to the article talking about our last case and the explosion. Jessica says Stella will be lucky if nothing bad happens at her wedding with you around. Called you a jinx."

And boy, I didn't need anyone else's help to make me feel like a jinx.

"The others?"

"She compares your and Stella's love life. How you're both widows. Says it's suspicious."

"Okay, I've heard enough. I'm gonna pay her a visit. Let's see how she acts to my face."

"Again, be careful."

I dug through my backpack on the passenger seat, finding my stun gun. "Oh, I'm not the one who needs to be careful."

"I don't like this," he moaned.

"Don't worry. I'm telling Leo before I go. I'll touch base with you later."

"May the force be with you," he said.

I disconnected and called Leo. He answered on the first ring.

"I was just about to call you," he said.

"I'm headed to talk with Jessica MacInerney-Jones. Apparently, she's got some issues with Stella."

"Yeah, that's why I was going to call. We got access to Stella's phone records. There's some text messages from Jessica that aren't very nice."

"Can you send those to me and to Toby?"

"I can share with you: you share with Toby."

"You must think Jessica isn't a genuine threat if you're okay with me going over there."

"I don't. Sorry. But I don't believe in loose ends either."

"So you're cool if I knock on her door?"

"Yeah, I hate to ask you to bring her bad news, but maybe she'll know something."

"That's what I was thinking." I put Winnie into gear.

"Call me when you leave her place. I want you to watch the video from the door cam near Bruce's. Maybe you can identify this first guy."

"Can you send it to me? I can watch now."

"I'd rather do it in person."

Weird. "Okay."

"And Sam..."

"Yeah?"

"Keep that SOS button on hand, just in case. Toby just texted me some of her social media posts."

"I'm packing my stun gun too." It was time to have a chat with Jessica MacInerney-Jones. Having a plan felt good, productive. No matter how loud that clock was now ticking.

9

THURSDAY AFTERNOON

JESSICA LIVED IN AN AREA CALLED FELIDA. A SMALL town holding tight to its tiny community roots as the borders of Vancouver tried to swallow it up.

Her house was a two story, built ten to fifteen years ago, on a street that bordered a park. At first glance, the house appeared well maintained.

I pressed the doorbell. Moments later the crackling sounds of an intercom filled the space, and Jessica said, "Dear Lord, what do *you* want."

I looked around for the camera, as the doorbell wasn't a ring bell. "Hey, Jess...ica. I need to talk to you."

"No, you don't. Go away."

I found the camera tucked in the corner of the upper part of the door.

"Actually, I really do. I'm not going away. I have something important to tell you."

"Tell me now."

"No, this needs to be face-to-face."

"I'm not letting you in."

"Then I'll just sit here until you have to leave or some-thing. Or your husband comes home."

She laughed. "Good luck with that."

The intercom gave an audible click. I'm assuming that meant she turned it off. Jessica's porch was wide enough for two chairs and a small table. I took a seat in one of the chairs and angled it so she could see me with the camera. I propped my feet up on the table like I was settling in and had nowhere else to be.

When, in fact, the opposite was true. Sitting here doing nothing was killing me inside, but I couldn't tip my hand. I was sending a message. That speaking with her was impor-tant. That what I had to say was worth all this nonsense. I tried not to look at my watch. I watched a spider in the corner work on its web.

Why wouldn't she let me in? What was she hiding? Was Jessica capable of taking Stella? If so, was her husband in on it? My mind raced with all the possibilities. I'd seen enough true crime shows to think anything was plausible. They could have Stella tied up in a bedroom or something and were hustling to make sure I didn't find her. Jarod, Jessica's husband, was a PE teacher. And we all know teachers don't make a lot of money, so that was motive enough. Who hasn't seen a show where just behind the door someone was being held captive? Didn't the cops return one of Dahmer's escaped victims to him? Anything was possible.

Never mind Jessica and Jarod had a six-year-old. Since school had let out a few hours ago, I assumed she was at some aftercare or sport practice. When my niece, Cora, stayed with us while Rachel was deployed, Cora's schedule had kept us hopping. Nothing looked to be hopping here.

If they had Stella, if Jessica was staring at financial ruin, all the loose ends, like where the child was, would be explained after I rescued Stella.

"Oh, my word, Samantha. Go away." Jessica's voice popped over the intercom.

"Nope."

She grunted. "Fine, come around the back. The sliding door is unlocked."

I rose from the chair, hesitating slightly. Come around the back? My spidey-senses tingled. Danger! Danger!

I waited until I was at the side of the house, surveyed the area to find no other camera, and was out of view of the front door, before I pulled out my stun gun and flipped it on, keeping it close to my body so it wouldn't get knocked out of my hand. I placed my free hand along my waist near my secret pocket and the SOS button. I moved along the side, hoping to look in the windows, but all the blinds were closed.

The backyard was small and filled with kids' toys. A plastic pool, water table, a pitcher and bucket tossed and forgotten in the yard. The grass was high but not to the point of overgrown. And only in the back. The front was trimmed. Either someone ran out of time, didn't care, or a combination of both, and was doing the bare minimum to appease the homeowners association.

The blinds on the slider were drawn back, and I looked into Jessica's cute yellow-and-white kitchen.

Holy crap! The place was a mess. Dishes were piled by the sink a foot high. Plates with food caked on them were still on the table alongside a milk jug that looked half-empty.

I slid open the door and tentatively stuck my head in the room. "Jessica?"

"I'm up here," she called from above. "And before you come up, can you bring me the Gatorade from the fridge?"

I'd been in some weird situations before, all of them dangerous, with outcomes that could have gone wrong. This one, by far, took the cake. No pun intended.

I stepped over a trash bag and moved to the fridge. When I opened it, the wave of onion aroma made my eyes water. I held my breath and took out a bottle of blue Gatorade, grabbing it by the lid so I could swing it and clobber someone, should I have to.

I crept up the stairs, checking corners as I went. The house was eerily quiet.

"Uh, Jessica?" I wasn't sure which room to go toward. The master was at the end of the hallway. I passed the laundry room with its several piles of clothes.

"I'm here. Jeez, Sam, you're the most stubborn person I know." She was clearly irritated and in the master bedroom.

I moved to stand in the doorway and gasped at the scene.

Jessica was propped up in bed and hugely pregnant. Not large. *Huge.*

"I don't mean to be rude, but how many babies do you have in there?" I didn't even know she was expecting.

"Three! Can you believe that? Three. I've been stuck in this bed with greasy hair and smelly pits and no company except you."

"You mean today, no one but me today. Surely you have people stop by?" Though given the state of the house, I kinda doubted it. I was stunned by Jessica. I was not expecting this at all.

She rolled her eyes. "Yeah, Stella comes all the time. Cleans the house and even brought me this bottle of dry shampoo." She motioned to a spray bottle on the night table. "Like that's going to make me feel better. But do you think I'd let anyone else see me like this? I don't even want *you* to see me like this, and I despise you."

"What did I ever do to you?" Intense dislike was new to me. I thought we got along fine.

She crossed her arms over her chest; they rested on her massive belly. "You squeezed me out of Stella's life. Not that she objected though."

"I did no such thing. How long you been stuck in bed? Because I think it's making you crazy."

"Four months! And you're darn right it's making me crazy. I can't do anything. I'm going to pop any day now, thank the Lord."

"Four months? Wow." I was still standing in the doorway.

"Yeah, a stunning lifetime. Before that, I was so sick I couldn't even get out of bed. Then when I felt better, my doctor tells me I gotta stay in bed because my cervix is a wimp or something. So here I sit." She harrumphed. "No baby shower, no nothing but crap TV."

That struck me as odd. "Surely, Stella offered to throw you a baby shower?"

Jessica crossed her arms. "Yeah, but do you think I want to have something in here? Look at me. I don't want anyone to see me. What a stupid idea. I told Stella so. Can you imagine the pictures? I look like a beached whale."

Holy mood swings, Batman.

"I think you look great. You have three babies in there. That's amazing."

"Oh, shut up." She wagged her fingers for me to give her the Gatorade.

I did, and moved to lean against the bedroom wall. "Listen, you've been saying some mean things about Stella recently." I omitted bringing up what she said about me. "Can I ask why?"

Moments after stepping into the room, I'd moved Jessica to the bottom of the suspect list, though I hadn't fully ruled Jessica out. Maybe she had a crap ton of pillows shoved under that flowery moo-moo she was wearing. Maybe her ankles were just naturally swollen bigger than my bicep. Never mind that she'd been on the slender side before. People change.

"Oh, what? Stella's feelings are hurt? She afraid I might make her wedding look bad? Damage her reputation? Is that why she won't answer my calls?"

"You called her a black widow. That's a big insinuation."

Jessica slapped her hand on the bed, and tears sprung to her eyes. "My dad is dead. He will never know his grandkids. And Stella? Stella is just moving along, happily finding a new man. I can't find a new dad."

"Jessica, your dad died three years ago. I wouldn't say Stella was moving along blissfully. She grieved for a long time."

"Oh, you would say that. You're the person she wishes were her daughter. You're her maid of honor. Did you know she wouldn't even let me bake her wedding cake? Actually hired someone else."

"Are you even able to bake her cake? You just said you could have these babies at any moment."

She slapped her hand on the bed. "It is the principle that matters. She thought that by asking me to approve the flavors, it might make me feel better, but it was just more of an insult. Like you being her maid of honor."

"I'll happily turn that over to you." I moved to sit on the edge of the bed.

"Don't be stupid, as if they make dresses for a woman about to birth a bobsledding team."

Jessica was all over the place with her anger.

"As my mom would say, 'There's a lot to unpack here; shall we begin?'"

"What are you talking about?"

"When was the last time you saw Stella?"

"About a week ago, Sam." She held up one finger and waved it in my face. "Stella is the closest thing these kids will have to a grandmother, and here I am ready to pop, and she decides to get married and write me off."

"When's your actual due date?"

She glared at me. "I'll be forty weeks, six weeks from today. If I make it, that is."

Stella and Tom got engaged four months ago and immediately started planning the wedding. "You were how far along when she got engaged?"

"About four months."

"And on bed rest, then?"

Jessica shook her head. "They put me on bed rest a couple weeks after Stella asked me to be her matron of honor, right after the new year."

I smiled. It wasn't until I stepped into Jessica's room that I remembered Stella telling me Jessica couldn't be her matron of honor because of a conflict. But she had never told me what. "How come you've never posted online about being pregnant?"

Jessica shrugged. "Every day seemed to be touch and go, and we were—are—afraid that if we announce to the world about having triplets, something will go wrong. We've been trying for over four years and have had some heartbreak. I just couldn't risk it."

"So Stella knew and a few other people?"

"Jarod's parents and his sister. My sister. Stella said we were going to have a shower after the babies were home and everyone was okay." She looked hopeful and scared at the same time.

I couldn't tell her about Stella. What if it sent her into early labor? But then again I couldn't come back here with worse news than what I was keeping. I didn't know what to do. If Precious were here, she'd tell. She was a *rip the Band-Aid off* kinda person.

If Stella's kidnapping were to make the news, well then, that wasn't a good way for Jessica to find out either.

"Where's Jarod?" Maybe having reinforcements when I told her would be best.

"Addie has soccer practice, and then they were going grocery shopping."

I chewed my lip, debating.

"So what's this important, pressing thing you have to tell me?"

"Maybe we should wait until he gets home."

For a pregnant woman stuck in bed, she moved really fast. She grabbed me by the shirt and pulled me close.

"I'm in no mood. I'm hungry all the time, I have to pee every fifteen minutes, and I haven't slept in weeks. Don't mess with me, Sam, or I'll use that stun gun in your hand on you. Don't think I won't."

10

THURSDAY AFTERNOON-EVENING

I GULPED. NOT BECAUSE I WAS AFRAID JESSICA COULD take me, but I didn't want to be responsible for any harm to her or the babies.

"It's about Stella," I said while peeling her hands off my shirt.

She grunted, and her fisted grasp became a flat-palm push-off, almost knocking me off the bed.

"I don't care about Stella. She's dead to me."

I cringed at her choice of words. Though I knew them not to be true. Hormones and fear were wreaking havoc on Jessica's emotions.

"I don't think you mean that."

Jessica shrugged and crossed her arms.

I pressed my palms to my temples.

"Oh my word, Sam. What the hell is wrong with you?"

I blew out a deep breath and said, "I have something to tell you, but I'm afraid it might send you into early labor."

"Well, keeping me in suspense might send me into early

labor." She'd been about to take a drink but put the lid back on the bottle and set the bottle on the bed. "Just tell me."

"Uh, earlier today, Stella was..." I search for a softer word rather than kidnapped.

Jessica clasped her hand over her mouth, and tears sprang to her eyes. "She's dead, isn't she?"

"No!" I rushed to say. "She's not dead. At least we don't think so. But someone has kidnapped her."

"Kidnapped!" Jessica's face expressed the horrible way she felt. "Are you kidding me?" She clutched her belly.

"Don't clutch your belly; you're freaking me out. Breathe. Deep breath in, blow slowly out." I'd heard Stella say this a thousand times. And it worked. Jessica started deep breathing.

"Kidnapped?"

"Yeah, they asked for a three-million dollar ransom."

More tears sprang to Jessica's eyes. "We don't have that kind of money."

That's when I officially scratched her from my suspect list. "Tom is getting it. He's reached out to his banker already."

Jessica nodded. "He does seem kinda nice...Tom."

I went out on a limb and shared something that wasn't really mine to share. "Did you know Tom lost his wife and daughter in a car accident before moving here?"

She shook her head. "No, but he was always saying we should come around more. As far as he was concerned, I was Stella's family, so I would be his family too." She covered her face. "I'm such a brat. I said terrible things."

"Well, I mean, on top of all the pregnancy hormones, you're probably feeling the loss of your dad more right now, and with Stella getting married, well, how you've been acting makes sense to me."

"Does it really?" She looked at me through her fingers. Her eyes wet with tears.

"Sure. And you know Stella understands. She's amazing like that."

"You have to find her, Sam. I need her. My mom is who-knows-where, embarrassed that she's old enough to be a grandma so she pretends like we don't exist. My sister is across the country. Oh Lord, I have to call her and tell her about Stella."

"I'm working on finding her. I have a few leads. Maybe you can help me make sure I'm not missing anything."

"Whatever you need."

"Hand me your phone. I'll put my number in, and you can text me anytime. I'll text you or call when I know more." She handed me her phone, and I added myself to her contacts. Then sent myself a message from her phone so I would have her number.

"Can you think of anyone who would want to hurt Stella or might think she has a lot of money?"

Jessica shook her head. "We all got some life insurance when my dad died. I used mine to buy this house. Stella put hers into investments. Safe, no-risk investments."

I stayed for another hour asking questions and fetching Jessica snacks. We called her sister together, and Lauren had no more to add that might be helpful. Both ladies were distraught.

I called Toby from my car. "You know anyone who cleans houses?"

"Yeah, why?"

"I want to send someone to Jessica's house. It's a hot mess.

Preferably today. I think having someone there cleaning and making things fresh would be a needed distraction for Jessica."

"So she's off our suspect list? Care to tell me why?"

"She's pregnant with triplets and stuck in bed. That would leave Jarod to do all the dirty work, and between working full time and taking care of their kid, I don't see how he could do it. He's not that well put together." Saying Jarod wasn't well put together was being kind. The guy was a scatterbrain because he'd used up all his brain cells on knowing the rules to every single game known to man. Tetherball? Yep, can cite them with his eyes closed. Pickleball? He'd prefer to show you on the court. Never mind the popular sports like football and soccer.

"I have a friend. I'll see if she can go today."

"Thanks, Toby."

"Hey, have you seen the video yet, the one they pulled from the door cam?"

"No, I'm on my way to the station now. Leo wanted to watch it with me."

"Yeah, that's a good idea," he said.

I was in Winnie and had pulled up to a stop sign. I stopped paying attention to traffic, as something in Toby's voice was off.

"What do you mean that's a good idea? What's in the video?"

He sighed. "I dunno. Nothing. Everything. I just... I dunno. Call me after you see it."

A horn honked behind me.

I waved at the person in an apology and made sure I was clear to go, then drove on.

"Toby."

"It might be nothing, Sam. Nothing."

I wasn't going to get more from him. We ended the call, and I checked my phone to see if Precious had texted. She had, said she would wait at my apartment.

I voice texted and told her to go to the station as that was where I was headed, and Toby's comments had felt foreboding. If something bad was going to be revealed, like Stella maybe being hurt, I wanted Precious there.

The drive, twelve minutes tops, felt like an hour. Leo was outside the station when I pulled in.

"What's wrong?" I could tell by the hangdog expression on his face something more had happened. He handed me the keys to LC.

"He's ready for you to take him back."

"That was fast. How is that possible?"

Leo rubbed a hand down his face. "We brought in a tech from the Vancouver department to process LC. There're a million prints in there. No blood or anything. You're going to need to clean him as there's fingerprint dust and luminol all over the place."

"No blood?" I asked.

He shook his head. "We want to look at Stella's car."

I handed him the keys.

"Tom's request for three million triggered an alert with the FBI. They're on the way down from Seattle now."

"You knew they were going to get involved at some point." The FBI covered kidnappings.

"Yeah, I wanted a little more time before they and DB got here."

"DB's on his way back?" This was not good news for Stella's case.

"He's catching a flight out of Mexico now. We have about

six hours. The feds will be here before him."

"And we have, what... eight hours before we have to have the money at the reception site?"

"Yep. I'm not going to tell the feds about you. Remember when I said we would do things together? Now I have to cut loose from that. I'll have to be here."

I nodded in understanding. He needed to keep me under the radar because I wasn't as hampered by the law as he was. I could talk to Sticks and Stone without reading the Miranda rights.

Yet Leo was worried about me being alone.

I tapped the front of my hip. "Remember, SOS button. It's going to be okay."

"Come watch this video."

Together we moved toward the building.

"Toby seemed freaked about this video. What's on it?" The apprehension from not knowing was giving me a bellyache.

"I'm not sure. The first guy, we think we recognize him, but we could be wrong. I need you to look."

We went inside, and I followed Leo to an interview room. Precious was already waiting in the room. A laptop was on the table, open.

"Hey," I said. "Thanks for coming."

She pinched and pulled up a swatch of her leggings. "I wore my stretchy pants so if I need to kick someone's ass I'd have no restrictions." She made like she was doing a leg sweep. Precious occasionally went on dates with Lockett, who was a black belt. Now I know what they did on those dates.

"Have a seat." Leo pulled out one of the two chairs in front of the computer.

We sat, and he stood beside me. "Okay, watch this, and let me know what you think."

He pulled up a video and pressed play.

I don't know what I was expecting, but what I saw was exactly as Leo had described. Two guys at different times, albeit moments apart, went toward Bruce's house. The first guy I couldn't make out. The second was Sticks.

To Precious, I said, "That idiot has a palm-sized birthmark on his right butt cheek shaped like a bright-red egg."

"Gross," she said.

"You're not kidding."

Leo said, "You don't recognize the guy?"

I shook my head. "It's hard to say. He could be anyone. He could be Hue. He's the same height and build as Hue. There's a moment where he turns toward the camera, but it's a flash. Can you slow that down?"

"Yeah, I noticed the same thing. I had Toby do that since we have to use Vancouver's department, and they're backed up." He clicked another icon on the computer desktop, and a second video popped up. Only this one was screenshots pieced together. Leo clicked through until we got to the one-second scene where the guy in the ball cap turned toward the camera.

Precious and I gasped at the same time.

"Can you zoom in?" I asked, breathless.

"The quality deteriorates with each zoom." But he clicked the button twice, and the face became slightly larger and a tad more pixelated.

I leaned in. "Oh my God," I said. I must have said it a few times because Precious put her hand on my arm and broke the spell. I knew that face. The straight nose, the lips thinned in concentration. Though the ball cap cast a shadow over the eyes, I knew what color they were and that there was a scar close to the right eye. This was the man I'd seen sitting in the Tesla.

I looked toward Leo. "That looks like Carson. How can that be?" I jumped up from my seat, shaking my head in denial. "That can't be Carson. He's dead. Dead. People don't come back from the dead, and zombies don't exist. So that has to be someone who looks like Carson." I'd been feet away from this man earlier today. I wanted to check my photos against this image. The enormity of Carson being alive and having possibly been so close to him was staggering.

"That's what Toby said." Leo glanced back at the screen. "I didn't really know Carson so I can't say."

Precious was chewing her lip. She said, "I know someone else who might know. Send the pic to Lockett."

"She's right. Do it."

Leo sent the image to my phone, and I texted Lockett with the question, "Who do you think this is?"

A second later, his reply came in.

Lockett: When was this taken?

Me: Today

Lockett: Had you not said today, I would say Carson. That looks like Carson. But he's dead.

Me: Could it be anyone else? A brother? A son?

Lockett: Sure, a doppelgänger. But not a relative, as he didn't have any.

I put my phone on the table, then buried my head in my hands, my world spinning. Nothing in this moment made any sense.

"How could Carson be alive? And what was he doing at Bruce Rawlings' house at the same time Stella was being kidnapped?"

11

THURSDAY EVENING

I SHOOK MY HEAD IN DISBELIEF. "IT CAN'T BE CARSON. It has to be someone who looks like him. I mean, I know Lockett joked about Carson faking his death, but I never thought that was a real possibility."

"Except that you thought you've spotted him around town," Precious said. "If he is alive, then you aren't crazy; you did see him around."

"You thought I was crazy?"

She shook her head. "I thought stress was getting to you. Or it was a way you processed the grief. Whatever. But I really didn't *think* he was alive."

I gripped the chair. "You know, he better not be alive. Because after what he did to me, to this town... he's not welcome here."

"All true," Leo said. "And regardless of who this guy really is, Carson or not, we need to find him." His gaze caught mine. "I need you to find him. The feds will be here soon, and I have to handle that until DB gets back to town. Case Bruce's neighborhood and see if anyone recognizes this guy." He moved to the computer and pressed print. Some-where in the building, a large image of this man was printing up, and I was going to be stuck staring at it until we found him. Truthfully, I wasn't sure which was worse. Not knowing or finding out.

Leo's phone rang and he stepped from the room. I sank back into the chair.

"You look all shook up," Precious said.

"I *am* all shook up. But I'm something else." I tried to figure out what all I was feeling.

"You're something else because you're a different person now. Partly because of Carson setting you up as a PI, but also partly because you've decided to actually live your life instead of going through the motions. Even after Carson died, you could have just tucked tail and stayed the course, taking photos of babies dressed as lions. But you didn't, and that has nothing to do with Carson and everything to do with you."

This was Precious in her life-coach role. This was why she was so good at what she did and why she had clients up and down the West Coast and across the country.

"What do I do if it is him?"

She sank into the chair next to me and took my hands. "Sam, trust yourself. You got this. You'll know what to do then. You'll know how you'll feel then. But what you need to ask yourself is what you care about more right now? Stella or that Carson *might* be alive."

"Stella," I said without hesitation. That was a no-brainer and put all these feelings into perspective. I couldn't let the fact that this person might be Carson distract me. He might be a doppelgänger, and worrying if Carson was alive might be a waste of energy that would distract me from finding Stella.

Leo came back into the room. "Am I interrupting something? Do you guys need a few more minutes to talk?"

I shook my head. "Nope, I just needed a moment to get myself together." I bumped Precious with my shoulder. "Thanks."

She toyed with the coach's whistle she wore around her neck. "Of course. And I didn't have to use this at all. Sometimes my clients get so stuck inside their heads and need a metaphorical slap across the face."

"Well, I'm glad you don't need more time. Graycloud just called. He said Sticks and Stone are at the diner. I thought maybe you would want to get out there and see if you could talk to them." His attention was on me.

"How did Graycloud know we were interested in them?"

"I let him know and asked if he heard or saw anything to let me know."

Precious stood. "Let's go question these yahoos."

"Actually..." I stood. "I need you to go back to my apartment and work with Lockett and Toby on trying to figure out where Carson might be staying. If this guy"—I gestured to the computer—"is really Carson, then the fact that we know him has to be an advantage, right? Maybe that knowledge can help us find him."

She gave me a puzzled look. "You're going to Graycloud's alone?"

Graycloud owned a diner and motel that was situated high in the hills and sat alone. But its proximity to the interstate, just a handful of miles, gave me the peace of mind I needed to go out there alone.

"Yeah, I'll be at the diner. Graycloud will be there. No

one is stupid enough to pull anything near or in front of Graycloud. And, I'll bring back cinnamon rolls if he has any left." Because Graycloud made the best cinnamon rolls in the world. They were *that* good.

Leo said, "I'll print you up a picture, Precious. Just in case." He handed me the one he'd printed earlier. "Let me know when you get there and when you leave."

I tapped my hip. "Don't worry."

We parted ways, and I was happy to be back in LC. Not that Winnie was a bad ride. She didn't know me nor I her, and if I had to run someone down, I didn't want to do it in Stella's car. Too much unknown with an unfamiliar car. With LC, I knew all his buttons. Like, right now, how touchy the brakes were. Anytime LC got an upgrade, he liked to milk it, show off whatever was new.

The drive to Graycloud's diner took twenty minutes. For a hot minute I thought I was being followed, but just as my heart rate started to increase, because the car was making all the extra turns I was, the car turned off. The hour was late, and the night was dark. The back roads to Graycloud's weren't lined with streetlights. When I pulled into the parking lot, Stone's Bronco was there. I took the flashlight from under my seat and shone it in the windows, looking for signs of Stella or a passenger who might have been kept in the cargo space.

I came up lacking.

Tucking the flashlight in my messenger bag next to my stun gun, I entered the diner. Graycloud nodded at me.

"Can I get two cinnamon buns to go, please?" I asked as I scanned the diners. Sticks and Stone were in a booth in the corner.

"Tread lightly, Sam," Graycloud warned.

I grabbed a chair as I passed a table and dragged it up to the end of the booth, flipping it backward as I straddled it so I could lean against the back. "Evening, fellas," I said.

Stone had a full head of hair that was heavily caked with product to make it stick up in spikes. He narrowed his eyes at me. "What you want?"

"How is it you know Stella MacInerney?"

Stone looked at Sticks. "You heard of anyone by that name?"

Sticks had longer, stringy hair but the straightest, whitest teeth I'd ever seen. He gave an open-mouthed grin. "Ain't never heard of her. Couldn't pick her out in a crowd."

"Well, you wouldn't have to. She was all alone at that house when you grabbed her. That makes her pretty easy to pick out."

Sticks laughed. Stone followed.

Stone said, "You've got it all wrong. I don't know what you're talking about, but we ain't been grabbing anyone. We don't touch women unless we have their express consent."

I gave an incredulous snort. With sarcasm, I said, "Oh, I'm sure that's one-hundred percent true. I was there, fellas. I saw your Bronco out by Bruce Rawlings' house. And you saw me. Your Bronco has the same drive belt as mine, and I recognized its squeak. I watched you roll by the house not once but twice." I held up two fingers.

Stone shook his head. "We didn't do anything, and we didn't see anything."

I'd been slouched forward, against the chairback, trying to be all casual. "Who said anything about seeing something?"

They looked at each other. Sticks said, "Why don't you get lost, skank."

It was a poor attempt to scare me. What I noticed was they'd stopped drinking their coffees, and Stone clutched the mug tightly.

"I'm not afraid of you. Either of you. I kinda feel like we know each other. Like we can be honest with each other. I have, after all, seen your butt, Sticks, and know you have a birthmark there. I feel like that connected us. And you did give me the slip. That was a good move. One I'll probably use in the future."

Stone leaned back and rested an arm against the back of the booth. "That was you?"

I nodded.

"You didn't do such a bad job yourself. we tried to get you to rear-end us."

"Thanks," I said and grinned. "I'm kinda new at this." I was hoping by being this casual and nonchalant, it would lower their defenses. They didn't strike me as the brightest bulbs, and flattery went a long way with most people. I hoped that would be the case with them.

Sticks leaned forward. "Listen, we was just cruising by, and the garage was all open and shit. We thought, hey, it must be a garage sale except everything was free. Know what I mean?"

I kept my expression blank. "Yeah, sure. Only a woman was taken and not any goods."

He held up his hands. "I'm gonna tell you only because we're sick of cops hassling us. You're the second one today. First, we get pulled over for something stupid like expired tags. Which they ain't, but whatever. He was just being a dick. And then you say we took a woman. Nah, we had nuthin' to do with that. You just think because we don't look like you think we should that we're bad or sumthin'. Man, I'm sick of it."

"I'm not a cop," I said. "I'm Samantha. Samantha True."

"We know who you are, bitch. Why you riding our asses?"

He pushed up his sleeves. His way of trying to intimidate me, only his arms were covered with several three-by-one-inch scars. Some old and white, some light pink and healing. Some ran across his wrist and onto the back of his hand. They looked like burns. Like someone had taken a hot iron to his forearm and hand. I glanced at the other arm and hand, and there wasn't a scar to be found. He made two fists, only the one with the scars couldn't close all the way, and then pounded them on the table once.

I wasn't worried about them getting rough, not with Graycloud around. But I wanted to make sure I left before them. I didn't want to get jumped in the parking lot.

I put my hands up in apology. "I don't want trouble." I dug in my messenger bag and pulled out two twenties. I threw them on the table. "As an apology, I'll buy your dinner." I motioned to the money. "What I want is the woman that was taken, and I think you guys can help me." I pointed to the burns. "Those look painful."

Sticks puffed out his chest. "They ain't nothing. You should see Stone's legs. They're worse."

I couldn't imagine.

"How?" I asked.

Sticks said, "The B Brothers. They like to leave a mark on you when you owe and haven't paid up."

"Why are yours on your arm and his on his legs?"

"It's how you fight. I like the punch," Sticks said.

I filed that away as helpful information just in case. I said to Stone, "And you kick?"

Sticks laughed.

Stone said, "Shut up."

Sticks said, "He likes to run."

I nodded to Stone. "I'm with you. I'd run too. Who are the B Brothers?"

Sticks said, "None of your effing business."

"If they grabbed my friend, then they're my business. Help a girl out. I paid for your food." They clammed up tight. "Just one little clue?" I showed them my thumb and index finger half an inch apart. "A tiny one. Maybe where I could find these brothers?"

Stone rolled his eyes. Sticks said, "Find Alonzo Prescott, and you'll find the B Brothers. They work for him." He made like he was zipping his lips.

"Alonzo Prescott? He some mob boss or something? Was he the reason you grabbed Stella?"

Stone shoved his coffee cup away and leaned in toward me, glaring. "We didn't grab your friend. Why not find the dude in the dark sedan."

I perked up. Did he mean the dark Tesla? "Was he wearing a ball cap and jeans?"

Sticks shook his head. "No, a ski mask and tracksuit."

We hadn't seen that guy on the video. Which meant either we missed something, or these guys were feeding me a load of crap. But I knew my time was almost up, and I was pushing my luck.

I stood. "Thanks for the chat, fellas. Next time you see me tailing you, don't waste a good shake by tossing it out the window. Enjoy your dinner."

I hustled off before they could say more. I paid for my

cinnamon rolls and beat feet to LC. I wanted to be locked in and driving away before anyone could catch up with me. And that's just what I did. Sticks and Stone were still at the booth when I pulled out.

In hindsight, I should have taken the interstate, but my habit was to take back roads. I was a mile from Graycloud's when I noticed a car behind me, using only fog lights. I tapped LC's brakes. He jerked to a slow. The car behind me did as well even though there was more than two car lengths between us.

I hit the gas, and LC lurched forward and took off, swaying from side to side as we took the curves ten miles per hour faster than we should have. The lights on the car behind me turned on and it sped up. When I was going the speed limit, a sedate thirty-five, the car had felt comfortable following me in stealth mode. But now that I was flying down the curvy road, the car needed its lights.

I took the curve, a sharp S-turn where trees occluded any oncoming cars and offered cover from behind. Around the second bend, I pulled onto the shoulder, slammed on my brakes and turned off my lights, bracing myself for impact. There was no telling what the vehicle behind me would do. He came around the bend at a high speed and nearly clipped my tail, but came to a screeching stop five feet ahead of me.

It was the dark Tesla. The one I'd seen at Stella's. Could this be Carson or his doppelgänger, or could it be the ski-mask guy?

The Tesla's fly door lifted open and out stepped a guy wearing a ball cap. It was the man from the picture that was currently on my passenger seat. I reached into my messenger bag and pulled out my stun gun, flipping it on.

I stepped out from LC and paused.

He put up his hands. "Let me explain, Sam."

Carson.

Seeing him was a gut punch. My senses reeled. The last year's chaos, the anger, fear, uncertainly, near-death experience and everything else slammed into me, much like the force of a fiery explosion.

"Oh, you think this is something you can explain?" I marched right up to Carson, looked him in the eye, jabbed my stun gun into his stomach and pressed the button.

He collapsed like a sack of rotten potatoes. And man, watching him drop felt good.

12

THURSDAY EVENING

When Carson regained consciousness, I was leaning over him, my stun gun close to his face, my finger on the trigger.

I waited for the fog to clear from his eyes before I said, "Think wisely about what you say. I desperately want to use this on you again, and what you say will determine if I do or don't."

He licked his lips and blinked a few more times. "Please don't.

Okay, I couldn't really shock him for saying please don't.

He continued. "I think if you did, I might piss my pants."

"Now, why did you go and say that? That makes me want to do it again." I put the prongs to his belly.

"Please, Sam. I can explain everything."

I shook my head. "Nope, I don't like that either." I pulled the prongs two inches away from his body and pressed the trigger. The electricity popped and cracked in the space. A loud buzzing followed.

Carson flinched even though I hadn't shocked him.

I let go of the trigger, finding the flinch satisfying. I mean, after all, that's what I've been doing since he pulled his stunt. Flinching. Flinching from relationships, from confrontation, from all the emotions that came with being lied to and taken advantage of.

"I hate you," I said.

"I know." He stared at me. "You should."

"I don't need your permission to hate you. In fact, I take it back. I don't hate you. I hate how much of a sucker I was. How easy it was for you to trick me. That's what I hate."

"You shouldn't be mad at yourself for that. It's because you're a good and honest person that I was able to do what I did."

"Oh, shut up." I waved the stun gun in his face.

"But you like being a PI, right?"

I jabbed the prongs under his chin. "I said shut up. You don't get any credit here, Carson. I decided, based on the options in front of me. I did the work. You get that?"

He gulped and barely nodded.

"Good." I stuck the stun gun in my back pocket. "Get up. I'm taking you to the police. And you're not going to fight me because you owe me. You owe me, like, one thousand favors, so essentially you have to do everything I say. Forever."

He raised his hand as if asking me to help him up. I slapped it away and moved to his car. I knew Teslas didn't have keys or fobs, so I was looking for his phone or the key card that he used to control the vehicle. I found the key card in the center console. Which meant he used the app to start the car. Though a cell phone was nowhere to be seen.

Carson was on his knees gathering his wits when I went back and patted him down, coming up empty.

"Where's your phone?"

"I could use some water."

"And I could have used the truth. Where's your phone? I can't have you running off on me."

He dug in his front pocket, pulled out his phone, and tossed it on the ground. Yeah, I hadn't patted there. Too awkward.

"Tell me what you saw today with Stella. Why were you even there?"

He crawled to LC, which was closer. With one hand on LC's door, he shifted his weight to that hand and pulled himself to stand. "I thought I was following you."

"How did you make that mistake?" I mean, Paulie Bee, my sorta PI mentor, said rule number one was to make sure you have eyes on the tail before you start the actual tail. Carson, being in security all his life, should have known that.

"I didn't figure you'd loan out LC."

His reply made me realize he hadn't been waiting outside somewhere for me to leave the newspaper office, or else he'd have seen Stella get into LC. "So you have a tracker on LC?"

"Yeah, I figured the odds were low it wouldn't be you."

I was at a crossroads. Pissed that he was tracking me and relieved that he was, because maybe what he saw could help us find Stella.

"What did you see?"

He leaned against LC, slightly bent at the waist, like he wasn't fully back to himself yet and spat on the ground. "Two crews. One in a black sedan and one of the guys in a ski mask. That's who grabbed Stella. She put up a good fight, but she took a blow to the head, which knocked her out. The other crew was the guys in the Bronco you just talked to. But I'm sure you know that."

"You get a license plate number from the sedan?"

He shook his head. "It happened fast. The greasy-haired guy, he was coming up the walk."

"That's Sticks."

"Whatever, he was coming up like he was up to no good. So I parked and got out of the car, ready to run interference. Then a masked man comes from inside the house and runs to Stella, grabbing her. Happened in seconds. I got ten feet before he'd subdued her and was bolting back into the house. I figured he exited out the back door. I ran to my car to follow, but when I got around the corner, I only caught the tail end of their car as it turned away at the end of the street. No license plates. Black luxury sedan, maybe a Lexus."

What he said would explain why the neighbor's door cameras caught little on Bruce's street. We needed to get cameras from the other street.

"Get in LC. I'm taking you to the police. You need to tell this to Leo."

"I'd rather not. Seeing as how I'm not even supposed to be alive."

"We caught you on a neighbor's door camera. And a lot of people have seen it and are wondering if you're alive or not right now."

Carson swore.

"How else did you figure I learned you were alive?"

"I thought you made me when you were at the scene. You took pics of me and my car."

"I couldn't get a clear picture. Too much shadow."

"I can't be alive, Sam. Your safety depends upon it."

I rolled my eyes. "Don't give me that crap. *Your* safety depends upon it."

He straightened. "You're right, it does. But a while back, I caught wind of a rumor that Copper put a hit out on you, and from what I've found out so far, this rumor has teeth. Austin Strong—"

"Is dead." My investigative work had put Austin in jail a few months ago, but he'd been fatally stabbed before his trial.

"Yeah, but before he died, he made contact with Cooper over their shared hatred for you, and don't think for a second that Cooper can't get something like this done from prison, because he can."

The problem with what Carson was saying was that I knew he could be telling the truth. But also, I knew this could be the perfect con simply because of its plausibility.

"Maybe I'll show Cooper the video of you. I'm sure that'll direct his attention off me to you." Joe Cooper had been Carson's business partner in Carson's real life. And in Carson's real life, he'd double-crossed Cooper. In his fake life, that's the one that I was a part of, I didn't know Joe Cooper existed until he came after me when Carson "died," thinking I was part of the whole takedown.

"Maybe for a second, but Coop takes pride in his ability to multitask. He'd just come after both of us at the same time. If he doesn't know I'm alive, then you have a secret weapon."

I stared at the man I knew as Carson Holmes, but whose real name was Jake Carson. I didn't know this person even though so much about him was familiar. Even though I knew how he liked his steak cooked and what knocked his socks off in the bedroom, what I didn't know was if any of what he was saying was real. If he could be trusted. And from there, what was the right thing to do? I played with the trigger on my stun gun, wondering if I shocked myself, if it would be easier than dealing with all this. Probably.

I traded my stun gun for my phone and called Leo. He answered on the second ring.

"Whatcha got?"

"Someone you need to talk to," I said while looking at Carson. He shook his head and stared at his shoes. "But he can't come in. You need to come to us."

"He? By any chance is this the guy in the video?" Leo's voice was low.

"Yeah, and if you can keep that video to yourself, that would be great." Carson's head jerked up. He stared at me.

"Sam, you know I can't purposely omit information pertaining to the case."

"Just for now, until you hear more; then you can do whatever."

Leo was silent. Through the line, I heard a door close, and then he said, "The feds are here and talking with Tom. They're gonna ask for everything we have any minute now. I want to bring them up to speed before DB gets here. You know once that happens, this investigation will become a shit show."

"If you decide to share it later, then tell them then that we only just acquired it. And besides, I'm sure some information has been withheld before on other cases because it plays a bigger part in another case or a pending crime."

"A pending crime? Good grief, Sam. Where are you?"

"We're on the back road leaving Graycloud's, headed back into Wind River. About one mile south of Graycloud's."

"Give me twenty minutes. You think you'll be okay until I get there?"

"It's not me you should worry about." I glared at Carson. Between the sliver of moonlight and lights from our cars, I could see his lips twitch as he suppressed a smile.

Leo and I disconnected. I went to sit inside LC. I called Toby.

"Hey, do me a favor. Make sure that video of the dude that looks like Carson doesn't leak out, and no copies are made. Can you do that?"

There was a moment of silence. "Does a bear crap in the woods?"

"Toby?"

"Of course I can do that, but why would I? If Carson is out there, and he knows about Stella, then we need to find him."

I didn't want to tell him Carson was alive and standing in front of me. That was something for a face-to-face. But I also didn't want to tell him or Precious because I worried that having that knowledge could get them killed too. Just as much as their association with me could. The thought gave me a stomachache.

"And we will find Stella, but there might be a bigger issue to consider too. And I'll explain all of that in person."

He groaned with unhappiness. "Okay, give me a list of who has the video."

I shared the names of who I thought might have it and who I knew had it. "Also, Toby, can you look into someone named Alonzo Prescott? He's associated with the B Brothers. Dig up what you can on all of them, but be careful."

From the side of my eye I caught Carson straighten, his focus fully on me.

"Dudette, I'm always careful."

We disconnected.

I said, "What was that? Why did the B Brothers catch your attention?"

He shrugged.

I held out my stun gun. "I'm desperate to use this again on you. Don't be an idiot and think by leaving me clueless you're helping me."

"It served you in the past. Like when I died."

"It didn't though, did it? I was almost killed. Both Toby and Leo were shot."

He sighed and stuck his hands in his front pockets. Then rolled his head as if he were stretching his neck. This was something he did as he weighed his choices. I learned the tell early in our time dating and used to find it endearing.

"There's a possibility that a contract on you would be carried out by the B Brothers. Word is Prescott accepted the contract and was putting his best men on it, the B Brothers."

I rolled the information around in my head. "We should wait and say all this when Leo comes. It'll be better than having to repeat it."

Carson cleared his throat. "You trust this guy, Leo? I know you've been spending a lot of time with him, and I know his brother is your best friend and he's your friend, but do you trust him?"

Without hesitation, I said, "Yes, yes, I trust him. And he's not just my friend, he's my fiancé."

13

THURSDAY EVENING

A<small>LL RIGHT, SO</small> I <small>LIED ABOUT</small> L<small>EO AND</small> I <small>BEING ENGAGED.</small>
I wanted Carson to know there was nothing between us
anymore. Someone else had filled that spot. Even if that
wasn't the full truth. But I figured if I could be Leo's fake
fiancée, he could be mine. And if I were going to tell this lie,
now seemed like as good a time as any. Funny how Leo and I
both had exes in our past making us feel these extremes were
necessary.

Carson pushed off my SUV and straightened.
"Engaged?"

"You seem surprised. I thought you were watching me."

He crossed his arms. "Yeah, not twenty-four seven, but
you two don't seem like people who are madly in love and
about to tie the knot."

I snorted in disgust. Like he would know "madly in love."

"Well, I'm only coming from experience. In Vegas we
couldn't keep our hands off each other, and the idea of
forever sounded so good, we got hitched right then and there,
remember?"

"I remember you not mentioning how us tying the knot wasn't going to be legal or real because you were already married. Never mind that you were using a bogus ID as well. And I also remember having had more than enough to drink. So I'm not sure what we did one stupid night in Vegas to what Leo and I are doing is an equal comparison."

He stepped toward me to say something, but I interrupted by sliding out of LC. I looked down the road to headlights headed our way. "Here comes Leo."

I went to lean back against LC when the first shot rang out and zipped over our heads.

"Jeez, maybe Leo's not who you think he is either," Carson said, straightening.

A second shot took out Carson's driver's side headlight.

"Get down," he yelled, running toward me. But I'd already hit the ground and was rolling under LC, my skirt getting caught underneath as I scrolled through options in my head.

Carson dropped to the ground and stuck out his hand. "Give me my phone. I need a weapon. I need to get into my trunk."

From my pocket, I pulled out his phone and tossed it to him. Another shot took out his other headlight.

"Wow, your boyfriend must really hate me."

"Leo isn't doing this, idiot."

"Sam, I want you to run back to Graycloud's; stay in the shadows of the trees. Go." He barked out orders, then scurried off to his car. A third shot took out LC's driver's side headlight.

I had to give the shooter props, because hitting these targets three out of three times while in a moving vehicle wasn't easy. Assuming those were his targets.

I wasn't about to run. I was pissed off. Angry that someone had snatched Stella. Angry that Carson had pulled a second ruse on me. Angry that these idiots were shooting at me and had damaged LC. I rolled to the other side of LC, and into the grassy ditch. There I crab-walked to the back of my Wagoneer and popped the tailgate. A while back, Leo had put in a roll of spike strips. His instructions were to use those to get away. He'd also loaded me up with mace, a second stun gun, and a body-armor vest. Yeah, he was worried about me.

I'd tossed a dark hoody back there as well and pulled it on, covering my light shirt and hair. I grabbed a pair of black slip-on sneakers and traded out my Mary Janes for those. Another shot rang out and ricocheted off Carson's car. He swore. There wasn't time for the body armor. It was buried beneath too much other stuff. I made a mental note to change that in case I needed it another time.

The car was almost upon us, and I figured they planned to drive by and rain copious amounts of bullets on us. They were taking out our lights to disorient us, limiting our abilities.

A loud succession of booms rang out near me, drawing my attention to Carson. He was returning fire with a handgun that packed such power, fireballs shot out the barrel with every round. When there was a pause in the sound I yelled, "I'm throwing a spike strip. Get ready to fight. Cover me."

"No, Sam, just run," he yelled.

And I did. I ran right across the road, unrolling the strip as fast as I could. Carson unloaded more rounds in the car's direction. Asphalt shot up around me as bullets danced near my feet, inches away. I finished the strip and dove into the grass, tucking and rolling to reduce any injury from impact.

Once I landed, I made a mad dash for the trees, knowing I needed more cover than Carson. Shots rang out around me. The only time I'd heard this many guns firing was at the shooting range with Leo. I made it into the relative security of the trees and leaned against one wider than me, muting the chaos from the road.

The sound of tires hitting the spikes, an explosion of air releasing, echoed through the trees. I peeked around the trunk. The dark sedan, maybe a Lexus, skidded from side to side as the driver struggled for control. I expected the car to stop.

That's when I realized my error.

If the car stopped, I had nothing to defend myself. I was a sitting duck. And I'd put Carson directly in the line of fire.

But the car kept going. I made out what I thought to be a guy wearing a ski mask, hanging out a window. He fired on Carson's car and then LC before swinging his rifle toward the trees and laying a stream of bullets in my direction. I sank into the brush and covered my head with my hands, tucking into as small a ball as I could while bark, small branches, and other forest bits rained down on me.

The car continued to drive away on its flat tires. As I figured, they'd either have to ditch the car soon or drive back to wherever they came from, staying under forty miles an hour. This meant Leo could catch up with them. My money was on them calling in help and ditching the car, which increased the likelihood they'd circle back to us. We needed to get out of here.

I waited a few beats to see if the car was coming back,

then decided I didn't care and sprinted out of the woods toward Carson, yelling for him.

We'd lost a fair amount of what light we had. One of LC's headlights was still on but it cast only enough light to see the passenger side of Carson's car. From what I could see, there wasn't a body lying on the ground, but then again I could only see one third of the area. That left a lot unseen.

"Carson?" I yelled again as I stumbled onto the road and ran toward his car. A quick glance at LC told me he'd been shot up and my rage flared bright and hot.

"Carson," I yelled again, this time with more panic. I wasn't happy with the guy, but I didn't really want him to be dead. And certainly not because of me.

"I'm here" he said. His voice sounded... normal.

I caught movement from his trunk as I approached. He sat up in the middle of his trunk.

"Are you hit?" I tried to assess what I could.

"Nope, as they got closer I jumped into the trunk."

"But this car took heavy gunfire."

"Yeah, but I had it tricked out. It's bulletproof. That's why I jumped back here. I returned what fire I could, so between your strip and my gun we made some damage." He climbed out.

"I think they'll come back. We should get out of here."

"What about Leo?"

"I'll call him. It's not safe here."

Carson looked at LC. "I don't think you're going anywhere in that."

Both the driver's side tires were flat.

To Carson, I said, "I guess your tires are bulletproof?"

"Not exactly, but they're better than the average tire. I can get us out of here."

I ran to LC. I wanted to get what I could. My camera, messenger bag, my phone, and the cinnamon rolls.

"Car!" Carson shouted. I looked in the direction the shooter's car had gone and saw nothing. I looked the other way and saw headlights. No way was this the shooters returning. The car was coming from the wrong direction, but it was traveling fast. I found my phone on the floor of LC, intact. I called Leo.

"Sam," he said. "I might be late. I think I heard gunfire, so I might have to respond to a call."

"The gunfire was here, with me. If that's you coming toward us, turn on your light bar to blue." Blue meant cop on the scene. Yellow meant caution and could be a tow truck or something. Red meant emergency and could be an ambulance. I wanted the shooters to know if they turned around, a cop was on the scene. I hoped it would be enough.

The car headed toward us turned on its blue lights, and I collapsed against LC's driver's seat in relief.

"It's Leo," I yelled. To Leo, I said, "I'll fill you in when you get here."

Two minutes later, he pulled up and put his service vehicle in park, leaving it in idle. He turned on his spotlight and scanned LC. That's when I saw all the bullet holes in the body. Had I hidden in the cargo space, I'd likely be dead.

Leo flipped the spotlight off and got out of the car. "What the hell happened here? Sam? You okay?"

I walked toward him on shaking legs. "I'm okay. A dark sedan drove through and tried to use us for target practice." I told him about Carson returning fire and how I threw the spike strip.

Leo's radio crackled with a report from dispatch. Shots

fired in the La Keep hills, a mile south from Graycloud's diner.

La Keep was the town after Wind River.

Leo picked up the mic and reported that he was on the scene now.

I waved for him to not say more. He moved the mic to his side, then walked to the spike strip and picked it up, glancing at Carson. "So you've been alive all this time?"

Carson leaned against his car and crossed his arms. "Yeah."

Leo glanced at me, concern etched on his face.

"He has some interesting things to say. You should hear them before you say anything to anyone else."

"I can't wait for this," Leo mumbled.

I motioned for Carson to fill him in. He did, but not without hesitation and a cross look from me. Once he spilled everything, the contract and Stella, I shared what Sticks and Stone said about the B Brothers and Prescott. Carson shared what he'd seen at Bruce's, including the dark sedan and the ski-mask man.

"Came out of Bruce's house, you say?" Leo asked.

Carson nodded.

"And how long has this supposed hit been on your radar?"

"About a month."

I did some quick calculations in my head. It had been about a month since Strong was stabbed in jail.

"If it's been a month, why haven't there been any signs of attempts or something?" I asked. Maybe it was a dumb question, but if someone was going to get paid for killing me, why wait to collect?

Carson shrugged. "From what I have gathered, it's

supposed to look like an accident. That takes time to set up and get right."

Speaking about how I might die raised goose bumps on my arms. I rubbed them to force them away. "This is why I asked you to sit on the video. If I'm the common denominator in this case, then Carson might be a big clue, and we should sit on that for a while. Right?"

Leo crossed his arms and ducked his head in thought.

"It's better for Sam if I stay dead," Carson added.

"You can say that again," Leo mumbled. He glanced at me. "At some point we need to show the video, so we'll need a plausible explanation for who the guy is if we decide to keep Carson dead. But that's down the road."

"We have to decide on this, right?" I jerked my fingers to the cars, indicating that the gunfight was the immediate concern.

Leo nodded. "I might ask your dad to put something in the paper about this and say it's reported an unidentified person was taken to the hospital. People will assume it was you, Sam, when we have LC towed to Bob's, but the shooters won't know." Bob's Body Shop was in Wind River, and Bob was LC's mechanic.

"They'll be looking for confirmation," Carson said.

"Sure, and they'll waste time going to the hospital to get it. For now, it'll get Sam out of doing the money drop for Stella. If what you say is true, Carson, that could have been a prime time to take her out."

I wasn't connecting the pieces. "But that wouldn't look like an accident?"

"No," Leo said, "but you'd be a victim of Stella's kidnapping, and there would be no reason to think it was a hit. Or they might try to grab you too."

I buried my head in my hands and groaned in frustration. "I can't lie low or anything. Stella is still out there, and we have, what"—I glanced at my watch—"seven hours before the drop?"

Leo walked to me and folded me into a hug. "I'm not asking you to lie low. I'm trying to buy you time."

I rested my head on his shoulder, gathering my wits. I worked on deep breathing for a few beats.

Carson cleared his throat. "This is all sweet and everything, and maybe if the outcome of this is good, you all will invite me to the wedding." He laughed, but it sounded fake.

I stepped back, and in response to the puzzled look on Leo's face, I whispered, "I told him we're engaged."

"Ah," Leo said, sliding his arm across my shoulder and standing next to me. He turned slightly to whisper in my ear, "What are you gonna do if he doesn't leave? With Mariah, at least she lives far enough away, and the odds of seeing her again are slim."

"I didn't think that far. I wanted a barrier between us, and this felt like a good one," I said through one side of my mouth.

Carson came over to us and stuck out his hand, offering it to Leo. "Congratulations."

Leo took it. "Thanks."

"Okay, so where do we go from here?" I asked.

The moment hung in the air. Leo was first to answer. "I need to get in touch with Tupi. We need an ambulance out here for show. We'll also need to tow LC to the shop. You need to go talk to the landscaper. His wife says he's at the Riverfront Golf and Yacht Club in downtown Vancouver. He should leave around ten."

We had less than an hour. "And how am I supposed to get there?" I gestured toward LC.

"Carson will take you. He can watch your back. We'll meet up at your apartment when I've cleaned this up and you've talked to the landscaper that Tom outbid. Then I'll have to check in at the station."

I asked, "What about talking to the B Brothers? I'd like to know how they knew we were here. Maybe Sticks and Stone called them?"

"No," Leo and Carson said in unison.

Leo said, "Stay away from them. If what Carson says is true, we don't want you making things easier for them."

"What he said." Carson pointed at Leo.

"What if they have Stella? I can't just not look there! At least let me go find Sticks and Stone to see if they had any part in this?" I motioned to several of LC's bullet holes. My fingers itched to use my stun gun again.

Leo brushed a hand down his face. "When we swept LC before, we found two trackers."

"Yours and his." I jerked a thumb to Carson.

Leo shook his head. "I had taken mine off."

I clenched my fist. "Is everyone in the world tracking me?"

Leo shrugged. "Looks like it. But once the trackers were taken off, whoever was in that sedan needed to find you by other means. So I think you're right about Sticks and Stone turning you in."

"But they couldn't have known we were parked here on the side of the road."

Carson groaned. "Luck. My guess is they might have tried to run you off the road. It gets cliffy a few miles after this."

Carson was right. The road twisted and dropped off in a few areas.

"But they shot at us. That doesn't look like an accident at all."

"Nope," Leo said. "I'm guessing someone is gonna be in big trouble from deviating from the plan."

I crossed my arms. "I want to talk to those two twerps Sticks and Stone."

"No can do," Leo said.

"I'll look there," Carson said. "After I take you to the land-scaper, then home."

"Solid plan," Leo said.

I rolled my eyes and shrugged out from under his arms, heading for Carson's car. "You both are idiots. You can't hide me away forever."

"We can try," Carson said.

He so didn't know me.

14

THURSDAY NIGHT

CARSON AND I RODE IN SILENCE TO THE RIVERFRONT Golf and Yacht Club where the landscaper, Terry Wiesner, was reported to be. I did a quick internet search on this guy so I'd know what I could about him and looked for pictures so I could find him in a crowd.

As luck would have it, he was walking out as we were walking in.

"Terry Wiesner?" I said as I approached.

He was about the same age as my dad, late fifties, thinning hair, the beginnings of a paunch, but he looked like he was trying to fight it hard, like he exercised. His skin was tanned from years in the sun.

"Who's asking?"

I stuck out my hand. "I'm Samantha True. I'm a private investigator."

Wiesner's brows shot up.

I continued. "I have a few questions for you about the bid you put in for the city landscaping contract in Clark County."

Wiesner nodded. "Yep, lost that one to Tom Rawlings."

Thing was, he didn't seem too upset about it. "You're okay with that?"

Wiesner shrugged. "Not at first. I was ticked. But I was going through a bad spell. Now I'm good."

I stuck my hands in my pockets and with my chin motioned to the outdoor bar next to where we were standing. "You wouldn't care to elaborate on that, would you? I'll buy the first round." I really could use a drink.

He studied me. "What's this about?" Guess I would have to wait to get that drink.

"I can't really say, except that I'm looking into Tom Rawlings and just wrapping up some loose ends. You made some fairly bold and aggressive comments toward Tom and the city when you lost the contract."

"I did. Like I said, I was in a bad place." He sighed and scratched his head. "Listen, my wife and I are going to visit the grandkids tomorrow, so I need to get up early. I'm just gonna cut to the chase. At the time, both my parents had dementia, and I was managing their care. My wife lost her job, and our oldest moved out of the state. My focus on the business slipped a little. I needed that city contract to help me reboot. Then my parents passed within a few weeks of each other and I lost the contract. I said a lot of things I regret. But I've moved on. Hey, how did you find any of those posts? I thought I deleted them."

I shook my head. "Everything lives forever on the internet. You said you moved on? How so? Because losing a three-mil contract would be hard for me to move on from."

He gave a big smile. "Right, that's how I felt at first. But my wife got a new job working for the casinos, and through that, I landed a contract job with them. Works out to be over three million." He put his hands up as if to say, *Hey, it all worked out.*

If Terry Wiesner was lying, he was doing a fabulous job of it. I glanced at Carson to see if he had questions.

He asked, "Where were you yesterday around five p.m."

Wiesner rocked back slightly and looked up in thought. "I spent most of yesterday at the RV dealership getting our RV serviced and ready for our trip tomorrow."

Carson got the name of the dealership, and we thanked Wiesner for his time.

He said, "Hey, I don't know who hired you and for what, but if you want a character witness for Tom, I can do it. He's a nice guy. I'm looking forward to seeing him and Stella at the next Chamber of Commerce meeting."

I assured him if it came to that, I would look him up. I thanked him and we left.

In the car, I said, "I'm gonna have Toby do some more digging, just in case. But I don't think Terry Wiesner had anything to do with Stella's kidnapping." I yawned and stretched, my hand brushing something in my hair. I pulled out a twig. "Oh my lord. How long as that been there?" On the drive to meet Wiesner, I'd at least removed the dirt from my face but missed this.

"Don't worry, he didn't see it. I didn't until just now."

"Just drop me off at the back of my apartment. How am I supposed to get in touch with you?"

"Put my number in your phone," he said.

I opened up contacts and tried to think of the best name to list his information under. Asshat was too obvious. My thumbs hovered over the screen.

"How about you list me under security?"

I typed in John D. The man with no identity. Seemed

fitting. Then I put in the number he called out. I tested it just to make sure he wasn't lying and ignored Carson's eye roll.

"What other agenda could I have than to keep you safe?"

We pulled up behind the paper and the backstairs to my apartment. I opened the door and said, "You'll forgive me for not believing you. Please don't go far. I want to know what Sticks and Stone tell you, those cowards."

I didn't give him a chance to say anything else, just left him there with his door open.

Inside my apartment, Toby and Precious were working on various projects. Toby online, Precious listing all the facts from Stella's disappearance on the large hanging Post-it notes we'd used in the past to list out each case's facts.

They gave me questioning looks.

"Let me shower and get some food, and I'll bring you up to speed." Minus a few facts I'd omit. Leo and I agreed they didn't need to know about Carson yet.

"I made coffee," Precious said.

I gave her a thumbs-up and closed the door to the bathroom. I took the longest, hottest shower of my life. What a terrible, awful, horrible day. I let the water sluice down my face, but there were no tears. I'd have plenty of time to feel sorry that my life was such a mess when Stella was home, safe.

When I got out of the shower, Leo was there with takeout and had poured each of us a large mug of coffee. I'd changed into jeans and a T-shirt and took a moment to pin my little pouch to the inside of my waistband.

We told Precious and Toby about the drive-by shooting and the ruse at the hospital. We lied and said we didn't know if the guy in the picture was Carson or not because we hadn't found him. This seemed to satisfy them, or they were too tired to push the issue.

Precious had a giant Post-it note dedicated to the B Brothers. Darrell and Darren Berry were identical twins. They'd grown up in Portland. With a marker I retraced the area Precious had drawn a square around. "This is all that they've been arrested for?"

She nodded. "Scary, right?"

Two things were listed: shoplifting and disorderly conduct. She'd written a year beside each one. They added up to over twenty years ago.

I turned to Leo. "Why are people so scared of them that Sticks and Stone have scars from these guys and they barely have an arrest record? In fact, they don't have one. These"—I tapped the box I'd drawn—"happened when they were teens. I don't get it. Precious is right, it's scary that they've stayed off the radar."

"Just because they don't have a record doesn't mean they haven't been in trouble. Maybe the state couldn't get anything to stick."

"Maybe witnesses disappeared and the cases fell apart," Toby said.

"Maybe they have an inside man who makes anything and everything disappear," Precious said.

"Maybe we're all too tired and have been influenced by Hollywood. Movies have skewed our imaginations," Leo said.

I didn't point out that my dead husband was alive. That felt pretty Hollywood-ish. That I was pretending to be Leo's fiancée. Another Hollywood element.

I put up my hands in protest. "Wait, wait. That would mean who they work for is powerful, because if they snatched Stella, then they're the grunts, the ground forces, not the brains. Tell me about Prescott; I'm guessing he's the brains."

Toby's hands flew across the keyboard. "Not much to tell. He has a small record as well. Most of it petty crimes, assault from when he was a teen. Kept his nose clean once he was an adult."

"He's a vulture," Leo added. "When he first got started, I would see him at the casinos circling people who looked desperate enough to sell their souls. And if they made deals with him, they essentially did. Sell their souls. He's ruined many a family. All under the guise of being a businessman. He has his hand in many local businesses too."

I cleared my throat. "Addiction. Lies. That's what ruins families."

We let the silence fall around us. I stared at Precious's notes, searching for some clue. Something to tell me where to find Stella.

I said, "Looking at this, what is the common denominator? I don't see any connections other than Bruce knows Sticks and Stone."

Leo shrugged. "He probably knows Prescott and the B Brothers too. Every cop with time in does. Maybe not personally, but you know *of* them."

This sparked an idea. "Toby, who were the arresting officers for the B Brothers?"

He named two different people that none of us knew, but then again, I wasn't all that familiar with officers from across the bridge in Oregon where the B Brothers were from.

I shook my head in frustration. I was missing something, and whatever it was niggled at my subconscious, trying to shake loose. "What about the arresting officers for Sticks and Stone? Anyone we know?"

More keyboard clicking from Toby. "Our friend Leo here had arrested them back when he was a rookie."

Leo squinted and rubbed his forehead as if trying to remember. "For what, again?"

"Jacking a car, it looks like."

Leo rubbed his chin. "Yeah, I barely remember that. It was when I was riding with Bruce, still doing my field training, right?"

Toby nodded. "Looks like Bruce and these guys have had a lot of run-ins. One or two a year even up to when Bruce retired last year."

"Wow, they must hate him," Precious said. "I bet he's been a thorn in their side."

I collapsed into the chair next to the couch. "Yeah, so they hate Bruce. They have him on their hate list or whatever, and they drive by his house periodically looking for an opportunity to get even. Today"—I glanced at the clock—"yesterday, they drive by and see Stella and think that's an opportunity. Finally, their luck has turned. Whether it's to grab her or break in or both, they now can get back at Bruce."

"I like it," Precious said. "It doesn't seem like a stretch."

"Except Sticks and Stone don't grab her. Someone else does." I stated the obvious.

The air left the room as deflated as a used balloon. We were getting nowhere with this. I rubbed my eyes. "I get the feeling Sticks and Stone weren't working with the masked man. So we're back to the main question. Why grab Stella?"

Leo said, "If we're to assume that the masked man works for Prescott, then we have to wonder why he wants Stella. She doesn't gamble; she doesn't have outstanding debt. She has money in the bank, but grabbing wealthy people and holding them for ransom seems like a risky business move.

Not his typical MO. And Toby can't find anything on Tom either."

"He's squeaky clean, doesn't even have credit card debt," Toby said,

"And he has the money to cover this ransom demand?" I asked.

"And then some. His wife and daughter were killed by a drunk driver in a semi. The company the driver worked for paid out. He's never touched the money. His company makes enough that he doesn't have to."

I recalled the three-million-dollar city contract Tom had won. Yeah, he was a guy who worked hard and made money. Not that those types of guys didn't have issues. Some did and some didn't. Could Tom have a deep, buried secret we had yet to discover?

At half past four in the morning, I heard Dad come into the newspaper, housed below my apartment. "We should go down. The drop has to happen in an hour and a half. Are we ready?"

"The feds are, from what Oliver Gee told me. And I checked in with the hospital. No one has tried to see our fake Samantha."

I tossed my hands up in frustration. "Nothing is connecting. Nothing makes sense."

Toby stood and picked up his laptop. "I'm going downstairs. I hear your dad moving around down there, and I bet he brought in some good eats."

I met Leo's gaze. In just over an hour, this whole thing could take a turn south. As if it hadn't already. And we weren't anywhere close to finding Stella.

Leo said, "It's do-or-die time."

15

EARLY FRIDAY MORNING

Toby had been right. Mom was with Dad and she'd made enough breakfast burritos for a small army, and brought yogurt, fruit, and coffee. I help her set it out in the kitchen. Something Stella would have done had she been here.

"I couldn't sleep. So, burritos." She held up the casserole dish.

Wait until I told her Carson was alive. "I think I've only managed a few hours of sleep myself."

"Dad says you have little to go on?"

I shook my head, tears springing to my eyes.

Mom paused stacking cups and pulled me into a hug. "You know that it's not your job to find her. No one will blame you for anything."

Unless she was kidnapped because of me. And Mom's words weren't true. I would blame me.

Dad rushed into the kitchen. "Bruce and Tom have just arrived. I'm going to bring them back here, so we can all hear what they have to say."

Part of the kitchen had been set up for meetings. Granted, Dad's staff was small, and with a few more chairs pulled in from the bullpen, we would have ample seating. I went out to get chairs. Dad was leading the way back. Tom followed behind him. The man looked like I felt. He hadn't changed clothes, and I felt guilty for having changed mine. Bruce was behind him. He sported a fresh suit but looked just as tired. Leo, Precious, and Toby were behind them.

Mom handed plates to anyone who wanted a burrito as they entered. Tom waved off the food.

"You have to eat something, Pop," Bruce said, looking worried.

He shook his head sadly. "Not until Stella is back."

"Why don't you fill everyone in on what the plan is, Tom." This from Leo.

"The FBI have the bag and the money ready to go. The money is marked, and the bag has a tracker. The FBI texted to say Samantha can't do the drop because she's in the hospital, but there has been no response." He glanced at me nervously.

"Who are they sending in my place?" I asked.

He shrugged. "Some female agent. They figured a girl was less intimidating than a man."

He didn't have to say what I was thinking out loud. That this drop could go wrong because I wasn't there, yet here I was standing in front of him able to do the task. How could he not resent me for that?

Just as I was about to volunteer, Leo interrupted. "Tom, you understand why Sam can't make the drop, right?"

Tom nodded.

Bruce said, "Do you have any idea, whatsoever, who was shooting at you, Samantha?"

A dish clanked on the table beside me. I glanced at my mom, who'd fumbled the dishes. I gave her an apologetic look. I'm sure she'd never be prepared to hear something like that.

To Bruce, I said, "I don't. I have a few guesses, but they're nothing more than that. Can you tell me about Sticks and Stone? You seem to have had a fair number of run-ins with them."

Bruce's brows went up. "Surely you don't think it was those two goofs? I can't see them pulling off a drive-by."

"No, I don't think it was them. But I'm wondering what they were doing in your neighborhood."

Bruce didn't seem surprised to learn this information. Probably he'd already been told about them, the ski-mask guy, and the stranger in the ball cap who we now knew was Carson.

He said, "Maybe they have family or friends in the area? Weird coincidence. Who knows?" He scratched his face in thought.

Only my gut told me this wasn't a coincidence. Two sets of criminals converge on the area at the same time? Nah, there was an important piece of information we were missing here.

"What about Prescott or the B Brothers? What do you know about them?" I filled him in on what we knew about their arrest records and reputations.

Bruce clasped his hands, one fist in the other. "What you just said is basically what I know. When I moved to the other city's cop shop, they had a few more run-ins with Prescott than we did up here. He's slippery and has a talented and crafty lawyer on retainer. What I learned about Prescott is there is no beating him or catching him. He's always two steps ahead."

"I don't even know who this guy is. Why would he take Stella?" Tom said. He stood and paced the room. "I don't gamble. I don't owe anyone any money. I don't have any enemies that I know of. I've played by the rules. I truly believe I am an upstanding citizen. So why Stella? Why me?"

I hung my head in shame as I searched for something helpful to say. The guilt of any possible part I played weighing me down.

Bruce stood. He said, "Pop, you can't carry this burden. Even the FBI agent said this might not have anything to do with you. Samantha might be the root."

Mom rushed to Tom and wrapped him in a hug.

My head snapped up. "The FBI said that?"

Bruce grimaced. "Basically. Sorry, Sam."

Next to me, Leo straightened and stilled. I caught his side-eye glance and knew something was off, though I wasn't sure exactly what. Leo jerked and began patting his pockets.

"I'm getting a call. Excuse me a moment." He stepped out of the kitchen and moved toward the front of the newspaper office.

Having stood next to him, I hadn't even heard his phone vibrate.

"Speaking of calls, I want to call my staff and check in to see if they've discovered anything," Bruce said, then turned to his dad. "We have to go to the station soon, Pop. To get ready for the drop."

Mom had gotten Tom to return to his chair. He was holding a mug of coffee with trembling hands. A nod was his only response to Bruce.

Bruce stepped out of the room. I glanced at Precious,

wondering if she had anything to say. She shrugged and shook her head.

This situation had us all rattled.

Leo came back into the room. He stood close to me, and my dad followed suit.

Dad said, "I didn't want to worry your mother about the shooting. I was hoping she'd never find out."

"Mom finds out everything, Dad. I'll tell her about it when we have more time to talk."

Leo, keeping his voice down, said, "I have to go to the station. I want to touch base with the feds. I asked Oliver about the agents, thinking this could be related to Sam. He said they didn't think that was viable. Had this been about you, Sam, then your parents would have been called. The approach would have been different. I think it's time I fill them in on our secret." He gave me a knowing look.

I groaned.

"What secret? I thought I was to be in the loop?" Dad said.

I closed my eyes with resignation. "Dad, you aren't going to like this." I opened my eyes and made eye contact with him. "You can't tell anyone just yet."

Leo interrupted. "We think someone has put a contract on Sam's life. We think it might have been Austin Strong or Joe Cooper."

Oh, that secret.

Dad's expression told me he was processing the information. He tapped his chin in thought. "Who do we have that would carry out such a contract? I'm going to check the morgue."

"The morgue" was where notes and story clippings were kept or put in a file for later use as a quick reference. Used to be newspaper morgues were in the building, but with the decline of traditional print newspapers, morgues had moved online.

Leo grabbed Dad's arm before he could take off. "Look for anything on Prescott too. Specifically."

Dad nodded, then was gone. Toby stood suddenly and caught my attention. He was staring intently at the screen.

My heart pounded. "You got something, Toby?"

I had to ask twice before getting his attention.

"Maybe. I've gone down a rabbit hole, but I forgot my power cord and I'm about to run out. Can't get to the end of this rabbit hole without power."

"We have a spare. I'll grab it," I said.

Leo went to stand by Toby, and I left to grab the power cord.

Bruce was coming out of the restroom, his attention on his phone. We collided before I could react. His phone tumbled to the floor. We reached for it at the same time, and that's when I saw his finger. His index finger looked like it had been shredded and rebuilt. The skin lumpy with scarring.

"What happened?" I lightly touched his finger that was permanently extended.

Bruce looked at his finger and sighed. "Got caught in a rope. Shredded my finger."

I grimaced. "Sounds awful. And painful."

"You have no idea."

Maybe not. I mean, I survived an explosion. I had scars on my arms and shoulders from sliding down a gravel road because of the blast to prove it. But whatever.

Bruce fumbled with his phone, picking it up awkwardly with his damaged hand. The finger next to his index finger had several small cuts on the side. The phrase "death by a thousand paper cuts" came to mind. I didn't say anything, though.

"I have to go," Bruce said. "My security team found someone sneaking around Pop's house. I don't want to tell him. I don't want to worry him, but I need to go check it out."

"What about the drop?" I glanced at my watch. "That's happening soon."

"Take Pop to the station. He's supposed to wait there anyway. I'll meet him there as soon as I can."

I nodded. Bruce turned to leave. Acting on instinct, I pulled the tracker Leo gave me, out of my pocket and palmed it.

"Bruce," I said. He stopped at the front door, turned, and faced me.

I quick-walked to where he was. I had no idea what to say. I panicked slightly. I wanted to plant my tracker on him but had no idea how to execute the plan. So I opened my arms and attempted to hug him.

"Good luck," I said. "And don't worry. We have things covered here." It was the most awkward hug in all of history. Our bodies didn't touch, I bro-patted him several times on the back, but as I moved away, I was able to slip the tracker in his coat pocket on his left side. His nondominant side. Hopefully, he wouldn't find it.

"Thanks." He looked at me in surprise. Then he turned and left.

I watched him hurry away. Leo came up behind me.

"We need that power cord. Toby has stumbled onto something."

I think I had as well. "Let me ask you something. If you wanted to punish someone, to take away their primary way of fighting back, what would you do? Oh, and this person is a cop."

Leo's brow furrowed. "I guess one thing a person could do would be to take away the cop's ability to shoot."

"Maim their trigger finger, maybe?"

"Sure, why?"

"I think I might have found a clue to our missing piece."

16

EARLY FRIDAY MORNING

I took the power cord to Toby. Leo trailed behind me.

When I set the cord on the table, Toby glanced at me, then back at the screen. "I found a list of properties owned by Prescott, all hidden behind a shell corporation. Leo thinks we should look at them. Maybe that's where we'll find Stella."

I put my hand out to Leo. "Give me your cell phone. Or better yet, open that tracking app you have and see where my tracker is going."

"Why would your tracker be going somewhere with you standing right here?" Leo pulled out his phone and set it on the table for all of us to see. The app was open, and the blue dot was moving on the screen, heading out toward Gifford Pinchot National Forest.

"I dropped the tracker in Bruce's pocket. See if this tracker heads in the direction of one of those properties owned by Prescott." To Leo, I said, "We need to find the link between Bruce and Prescott." I shared what Sticks and Stone said to me about how Prescott liked to disable people's abilities to strike back. Like permanently damaging a cop's trigger finger and making him ineligible to be on the force. If a cop couldn't pass qualifications on the shooting range, a cop couldn't keep his job.

Leo stared at me for a moment, then turned to Tom. "I have a tough question for you, Tom. I'm sorry to ask this, but by chance does Bruce have a gambling problem?"

Tom shook his head. "No."

Okay, so maybe Tom didn't know about Bruce's gambling? I turned to Toby.

"I'm way ahead of you. I'm digging into his records now," he said.

Tom sighed. "Unless you want to consider start-ups gambling. Bruce thinks he's a savvy businessman, but he's a sucker for the next get-rich-quick scheme. Ever since he left the force, he's been looking for his next career."

"He's had a couple of misses?" I asked.

Tom nodded. "Expensive misses. I've bailed him out one too many times. I told him this last time, he was on his own."

Leo and I exchanged a knowing look. Perhaps Bruce owed some people for those misses. Owed them big-time.

Leo said, "Come on, Tom. Let's get you to the station. Bruce had to take care of something. He'll meet us there. Let's go talk to the feds about the drop." To me, he said, "You keep working on a link."

I nodded, then walked Tom and Leo to the door, trying to comfort Tom along the way. Once they were gone, I went back to Toby.

"Samantha Jane," Mom said. "You've got that look in your eye. The one that tells me something is about to happen."

"Mom," I said, pleading. "This is Stella. Please don't ask me to stay here."

She shook her head. "I'm not. I just want you to take some weapons with you. Something to protect yourself. A gun, a bullet-proof vest. Something."

"Okay, I will." I moved to hug her. "Leo and I have been talking about various safety options. We're putting a lot in place."

She hugged me back. "I just hope it's enough."

"Bull's-eye!" Toby said. "The tracker stopped moving at one of Prescott's properties in Cougar."

Cougar was a small town at the base of Mount St. Helens.

Precious jumped to her feet. "Let's go."

Toby stood.

"No," I said. "You have to charge."

"No," he said. "I have an adaptor in Precious's SUV. Left it there from last time."

"Don't say I didn't give you an out. You're always complaining about how your life is in danger."

My mother groaned.

Toby said, "Hyperbole, Elizabeth. And probably a little too much weed. For the most part, our trips out are dullsville."

"We're just going to stake the place out, Mom. See if Stella is there." I airdropped the destination to my phone, then handed Leo's phone to my mom. "Give this to Leo. Tell him where we're going. And can you reach out to Mariah, the wedding planner? I don't know if anyone has told her what's going on. Tell her we need to push the wedding back a day. Which means we need to contact the reception hall and caterers and—"

"I'll take care of all that. It'll give me something to do."

I smiled. "Thanks, Mom. Oh, and if Mariah says something about me and Leo being engaged, just roll with it. Pretend like it's old news. I'll explain later."

Mom's mouth dropped slightly open. "Engaged?"

I grabbed my messenger bag. "It's a long story. I'll tell you one day over dinner." I kissed her cheek. "Fill Dad in, too, please."

All she could do was nod.

Seconds later, we were out the door, in Precious's SUV and speeding toward Cougar.

"We need a plan," Precious said.

"We need backup plans for our backup plans because our plans always go sideways," I said.

"We should just wing it," Toby said.

Yeah, that's likely what we'd do anyway. "Let's assess when we get there," I said. I rummaged through my messenger bag, getting organized. Cell phone, stun gun, flashlight, and mace. Not much of an arsenal. Our plan, whatever it was going to be, was definitely not storming the building.

The drive to Cougar was forty minutes. By now the drop would have gone down. I glanced at my cell phone. Nothing. Cell service in the mountains was spotty. I texted Leo and asked how things were going, but I'd have to wait until we were out from these trees before I would get a bar of service.

"Okay," Precious said, pulling to the shoulder. "This is the turnoff. But I don't want to go that way in case the people there might be alerted that we turned into their drive."

"Good call," I said. "Just pull up the road a bit and pull onto the shoulder. We'll go on foot and cut through the trees."

"Ugh, why do we always have to hike? Just once I want to be like in *Die Hard* and be in a high-rise, one contained area." Precious put her hair in a high ponytail.

"I'm afraid of heights," Toby said. "That sounds awful."

"I have no interest in crawling through air ducts," I said.

"You both are buzzkills," Precious said.

"Listen, this is all I have on hand." I listed my pathetic arsenal. "Do either of you have anything?"

Precious opened the door to her cargo space. "I have a few blankets, a pair of binoculars, and a tire iron." She grunted. "I keep meaning to put tools of the trade in here, but I keep forgetting."

"Take the tire iron," I said. "And the binoculars."

I glanced around. The forest was quiet around us. The road not often traveled. We had about a little over an hour of darkness before we'd see the sun. I didn't know if that was good or bad.

I looked down the road we'd just come from and wondered if Carson was out there. Or if Leo was on his way. Standing out here under the shadow of Mount St. Helens, the fading night with the early morning sun not yet peeking out, with only Toby and Precious, left a sense of being alone. We were it.

17

FRIDAY MORNING

"Come on," I said. "Let's go see why Bruce came all the way out here and if Stella might be here."

We slowly made our way through the woods, keeping the dirt driveway to our left and using it as a guide. Our journey didn't take long before I could make out a small cabin tucked among the tall Douglas firs and Western hemlocks. The lights in the window and smoke from the chimney gave it away before I could actually make out the building. The copse of trees was thick, and any light attempting to break through was strangled out at the tops of the trees. Here inside the forest was like rewinding the clock to well before sunrise. But they offered suitable cover, so we got as close to the cabin as we could, about fifteen yards out.

We crouched behind trees, the darkness settling in around us, and watched and listened. Everything was still, the animals, the air. I breathed through my nose, afraid to disrupt the silence. I raised Precious's binoculars, trying to peer inside the cabin. A thin, sheer fabric covered the window, giving the interior a hazy filter.

I turned toward Toby and Precious, both behind trees on my right. I could barely make them out. An elbow jutting out from behind one tree, a shoulder peeking around another, both almost looking like knobs on the trunk and not parts of people.

"Psst," I whispered.

Neither moved. They weren't that far behind me. Max ten feet. They should have heard me. Or at least looked around to see who or what made that sound.

I gave a short bird whistle. If the little cabin had a guard patrolling who knew anything about nature sounds, my bird whistle would've given them pause.

Again, Toby and Precious didn't move. My heart raced. I leaned forward, straining to see them, wondering if what I thought was them were branches or something. Were they still there? I glanced around me. Had a guard snuck up and taken them out? I dropped to my haunches and swiveled, putting my back to the tree and cabin.

"Precious," I loud-whispered. "Toby."

"Sam?" Precious said.

"Are you both okay?" I asked.

"I can't really make out anything," Toby said. "I'm afraid to move."

I blew out a slow breath, steadying my racing heart. Again, the nagging fear of being underprepared gnawed at me. I tapped my fingers against my legs in thought. If I could get confirmation that Stella was inside, then I could send Precious and Toby to intercept Leo, who was hopefully on his way with the cavalry. In this case, the Wind River police force. Confirmation was all I wanted. Then I would wait it out.

A scream broke through the trees. Then a female said, "Leave him alone!"

I shot up. Stella. Thank heavens she was still alive. And from the indignant tone in her cry, unharmed.

She screamed again, this one heavy with anguish. "Please, my arm, you're gonna break it," she cried.

I sank back onto my haunches. Okay, maybe unharmed wasn't exactly accurate. I glanced at my watch. *C'mon, Leo. Hurry!*

But he didn't appear with help in tow.

"Sit down, you old biddy. And shut up, or I'll shut you up," came the reply from a deep, angry voice.

I crouch-walked to where I thought Precious was and accidentally bumped into her, knocking her back against a tree. I didn't dare turn on a flashlight. Any beam, big or small, out in this darkness would call attention.

Precious leapt away, drawing a full breath as if about to let out a scream, only instead she whimpered.

"It's me. Sam. You're okay."

"Lord, Sam, you scared me." She crouched down, and our faces were close. I could make out her features. Her platinum hair tucked under a dark cap made her face more ghostly and pale.

"I'm going to sneak ahead for a closer look."

"Don't do anything stupid."

"Like what? Hopefully, Leo will be here soon. I just want to see if there might be something we can do to draw them away from Stella. You heard what that guy said to her."

Precious sighed. "I don't like it. Something could go wrong."

I nodded. "Sure. But what if they hurt her again? Do we just hide behind a tree and listen?"

"We'll wait here," Toby said from the darkness. "Just take a quick look and come back."

I nudged Precious on the knee. "I can't see him, but I think that was Toby, or maybe it was the voice of reason. A higher power giving permission."

Toby snickered.

Precious grunted in irritation. Her way of agreeing without having to say it outright.

I tapped her again. "I'll be right back. If I can find my way back."

I didn't wait for more, just crouch-walked out from behind her tree, bent at the waist hoping to use the large ferns for cover. I bolted to the next tree. Which in hindsight was stupid because it's not like I could see the forest floor, and the odds of tripping over something were really high. I picked another tree about five yards diagonally from me with what I hoped had a better view inside the window. I crept slowly toward it, kicking my legs out wide with each step as a way to clear the space before me. On my third step, I got caught on something thin and taut. It stretched across the ground, about three inches from the forest floor.

I had an inkling of what it was. A trip wire. And in my sweep, I had stretched it. Meaning when I brought my foot back, the wire was going to relax and trigger. I balanced on one foot, my other still caught on the trip wire.

"Precious. Toby," I said in a low voice. But definitely not a whisper.

"Uh, yeah, Sam?" Toby replied.

"I want you to run back toward the car. Stay low if you can." I wasn't sure what this trip wire would trigger. The range could go from an explosion to an alarm inside the house. An explosion would draw too much attention and possibly cause a forest fire. And I didn't figure kidnappers for environmentalists—small-minded of me, sure. I'd been through an explosion before. They weren't fun. I rubbed the rough patch of skin running from my elbow to the wrist. Road-rash scar.

"What about you?" Precious said.

"I'll be right behind you. Ready?"

"No," they answered in unison.

"I'm never ready for shit to go wrong," Toby said. "You think I'd be better prepared by now, but I think I'm this naïve, hopeful optimist that everything is always okay with the world."

"Says the man with an emotional-support animal," Precious countered.

"Run!"

They crashed through the woods. I couldn't see where they were, but they sounded like a herd of deer being chased. I wanted to give them a head start, but I didn't want to give the guys in the cabin any more time than I had to. I counted to three and took off behind my friends. Bracing myself for an explosion.

What I got was not what I expected.

A flare shot up from the ground behind me and lit the sky in shades of red as it exploded below the clouds. Ahead of me I could make out Toby and Precious clear as day. I glanced over my shoulder, and a tall, heavily armed man was standing outside the cabin, the window light behind him haloing his silhouette. He aimed a semiautomatic rifle at us.

"Get down!" I yelled and dropped to the ground. "Gun."

Toby and Precious hit the deck. Seconds later, a streak of bullets rained over us, hitting trees and splitting off chunks of bark. I commando-crawled toward them, praying the flare would fade sooner rather than later. I reached Precious first. Because, let's admit it, Toby may be waifishly thin and vehemently opposed to physical activity, but in a pinch, that dude could book it when he wanted. Case in point, he was yards ahead of us.

"We need better cover." I scanned the forest. "They know where we are and when the flare fades, we need to not be here. Plus, the sun will come up soon."

Toby gave a short whistle. I looked his way. Second by second, the surrounding area was gradually getting lighter.

We made eye contact, and he jerked his eyes to the left, but from where I was, I couldn't see anything in that direction but ferns and trees. I was too low to the ground. And I didn't want to rise any higher for fear of getting shot. The gunman was waiting for me or any of us to do just that.

As if on cue, a spray of bullets flew to the right of us and pelted a swath of trees.

I looked at Toby and gave him three fingers, then pointed to my watch. Three minutes. The flare would be fully faded by then. Then using two fingers, I made them scissor quickly and hoped he knew I meant to run. I motioned toward me and Precious, made the fingers-running signal, then gestured to him. We'll follow you was the message. I hoped he understood. He nodded like he did.

We looked at our watches and marked the time.

"Get ready to move, Precious," I whispered. My thought was that we couldn't wait any longer. It's not like we would have full darkness to cover us. The minutes ticked away slowly. I half expected a guy toting a gun to stroll up to us; that's how long the three minutes felt.

Ten seconds to go. I glanced at Toby again and he gave me a thumbs-up.

"Get ready." I started the countdown. On one, we all jumped up, attempted to stay low, and dashed off to the left. A smattering of shots went out around us but appeared to fall short. Maybe they thought they'd chased us away? Toby led us to a stand of weathered trees. We all ducked behind it and sank to the ground.

"Why are we always in these situations?" Precious asked between panting gasps.

Toby blew out a breath. "If we get out of this alive, I'm going to get another emotional-support animal. The burden will be too great for Lady M." Lady M or Lady Marmalade was Toby's sugar glider.

Precious grunted. "I might get one myself."

"If we get out of this unscathed," I said, "I think I'm going to..." I mentally rolled through the options.

Precious chuckled. "If you get out of this alive, you should get a life. Do more than work at Click and Shop and this PI gig."

"And what more should I be doing?"

"Date," Precious said.

"Yeah," Toby chimed in. "You totally need to date."

If they only knew. I snorted, "Says the guy who doesn't date."

Toby stiffened. "Say what? I date. I date all the time."

Hopefully the light was conducive to witnessing my eye roll. "A scheduled time to get high every day and devour a bag of Cheetos isn't a date."

He huffed. "If there weren't men with guns near us, I'd raise my voice because I am insulted. I'll have you know I've been seeing Ruby the yoga instructor for quite some time."

"Wait, Ruby the instructor who had the studio next to Carson's office?" The first time I met Ruby was a year ago.

"Yep, that's the one."

Precious said, "How is it we didn't know this?"

I felt, more than saw, Toby shrug. "I like to keep my private life private."

"See, Sam," Precious said. "You need a life. Carson is dead. It's been a year. Time to move on."

"Yeah, about that," I said.

She groaned. "You don't really think the man in that video is Carson? Yeah, I did, too, at first, but the more I look at it, the more I think it's not. Carson is dead."

"Um, no he's not," I said. "I saw him yesterday."

"*Saw him* saw him? Or think you saw him, like you have in the past?" Toby asked.

"*Saw him* saw him. Used my stun gun on him. I wasn't sure how to tell you or even if telling you was the right thing to do. Maybe knowing this puts you in danger."

"Gee," Toby mocked. "It's not like we're ever in danger." He gave me an eye roll of his own.

I poked my head from around the group of trees to look for the guard. He was still on the porch scanning the forest in our direction.

"He's really alive?" Precious asked.

"Yeah."

Toby stuck out his hand. "Pay up, Precious."

She shoved him in the shoulder. "As if I have fifty dollars on me right now. Moron."

"You're just mad because you lost the bet." Toby looked at me. "I bet Carson was alive—and I won."

I scanned the area behind us, wondering if someone might try to flank us.

"Well, here's a fun tidbit. Carson also thinks Leo and I are engaged."

Toby and Precious gasped.

"I'm guessing you told him that. Any special reason why?" Precious asked.

"I wanted to be clear there was no place for him in my life. So if you see Carson, you have to keep up the ruse."

"It's not such a stretch of a lie," Toby said. "When you and Leo are together, we need a knife to cut the sexual tension."

I groaned. Precious laughed.

"What? Was that too much?" Toby said. "Okay, maybe it's not that awkward, but there's something there. You have to admit that."

Yeah. There was something there. But now I had to deal with Carson. Who, unfortunately, wasn't going to get in his car and drive away to Seattle, like Mariah.

"What a mess," I mumbled.

"No joke," Toby said. "Your personal life and this situation is the equivalent of a dumpster fire, and I would like to get out of this fire alive, so I can take Ruby to the Indian restaurant in Portland."

I checked the location of the guard. He was still at the front of the cabin, scanning for us. I looked around. No one appeared to be coming. I pulled out my phone and willed it to have a signal and some message but found nothing.

"Okay," I said. "I have a plan. It's awful and stupid. But I think it'll work."

18

FRIDAY MORNING

I PUT CARSON'S NUMBER IN PRECIOUS'S PHONE, THEN sent her back to her SUV to go off looking for Leo or any help she could find.

Toby had drawn the short straw, or in this case, twig. His job was to hunker down and cause a distraction while I attempted to skirt the perimeter of the cabin and get close. I needed to know how many we were up against.

From the forest floor, Toby and I gathered rocks and large sticks that he could use to toss. His goal was to throw these items in various directions to distract the guard at the front.

I crouched low next to him. "Remember, don't throw them in the direction I'm going. I'll be going right. Try to throw them as if a person is sneaking up toward the cabin in that direction." I indicated to his left. "Got it?"

"Nope," he deadpanned.

My mouth opened, but words were lost. "Uh..."

"Yes, I got it. Duh. Just go already. I want to go home." He pushed me to get me moving.

I smiled. "If we get out of this unscathed, *I* might need an emotional-support animal." I was stalling. Hoping to give Precious more time to gather the troops so I wouldn't have to do this. I was afraid I was gonna mess this up, and not only would I get hurt, but so would Stella. The thought was almost paralyzing.

He grinned. "You need a dog. Now, go." He jerked his thumb, indicating I should get lost.

I sucked in a deep breath, blew it out slowly, made sure my messenger bag was secure, then scurried off.

Daylight was pushing hard through the canopy of leaves. I had to stay low and move slowly. Ten yards later, I accidentally stepped on a twig. The snap echoed through the forest.

The guard turned toward me and stepped off the porch and into the grass, coming in my direction. Toby threw something in the opposite direction that landed with a loud thunk and rustling of foliage. The guard stopped and surveyed that area. His semiautomatic was raised and ready to fire. Holding my breath, I moved closer, trying to watch the guard and check for trip wires as I went.

The guard lowered his gun and surveyed the area. His attention returned to my direction.

Toby threw another rock. The guard looked back toward where the rock landed, then in the direction where Toby was hunkered down. The guard's head tilted sideways as if he was trying to make out something. I looked over my shoulder in Toby's direction and caught the slightest flash of bright blue. Toby's shirt. Blue was not a color common in nature. Sure, things tended to look blue, and there was the occasional blue flower, but nature didn't create those. People did. Toby's shirt was giving him away.

The guard raised his rifle and looked down the scope toward Toby.

I could only imagine Toby's panic, seeing the guard pointing his weapon at him. I wildly scanned the ground, running my hands over the dirt and plants, looking for something to throw. Nothing. I glanced at the guard. He widened his base of support, taking a step to the side, moving into a position to shoot. Time was up. The guard's finger was on the trigger.

I stood up and cleared my throat. "Excuse me."

The guard swung the rifle toward me, his eyes still glued to the scope.

"My name is Samantha True. I think maybe your boss might want to meet with me. We have business to discuss."

The guard didn't flinch. "Oh yeah, and what business is that?"

"That's between us. But you should go ask him if he wants to meet with me. I'll wait here."

"Nope, no can do. Tell your friend to stand up."

"What friend?" I attempted to look confused.

"In the blue shirt."

"That's not my friend. That's my backpack."

"Your backpack?" He was still staring me down through the scope.

I faked a laugh. "Yeah, I was kinda hoping to get Prescott alone. I've been waiting here for him to come out. I put my backpack there to help me find the road back out of here." I motioned to where Toby was hiding. "See, that spot runs parallel to the road. I guess you could say the pack is kinda like my breadcrumbs."

"Breadcrumbs?"

"Yeah, like in the fairy tale. They used the breadcrumbs to lead them out of the forest."

"Never heard it, but I can tell it's stupid because who would do that. Animals would eat the crumbs."

I gave a wobbly smile and wagged my finger at him in fake excitement. "That's exactly what happened. Too bad those kids didn't have someone like you to teach the ways of things. Now, how about that meetup with Prescott? Think you could get him for me?"

I desperately needed this guy to lower his gun. Soon my body was going to tremble from the anxiety and fear of having the weapon aimed at me.

As if he heard my wish, he lowered the gun, so it pointed to my belly or parts below. Not ideal, but better than pointing at my face.

"What did you say your name was?"

"Samantha True."

He jerked the gun to signal me to come toward him. I did so, albeit slowly. Picking my way through the brush, acting like it was harder than it looked. Stalling. I was totally hoping to put minutes on my side, not theirs.

"Move it, lady," Guard Guy grunted. "I ain't got all day."

I approached the guard so he couldn't see behind my back. I tucked my hands back and out of sight from him. But hopefully Toby could see them, and I flicked my hands, telling him to go. Run. Get away.

"Hands where I can see them." The guard lifted the rifle.

I moved my hands to the side where he could see them. Worried that Toby didn't get the message, I pretend a bug was swarming. I shooed and waved my hands wildly, saying, "Shoo, get away, leave me alone." I spun around, and when I was facing Toby, I said it all again, doing the crazy dance of a woman being pestered by a large bug.

"Lady, I'm gonna shoot you," the guard warned.

I faced him and gave a halfhearted attempt at my continued shooing. "Stupid bugs, they freak me out." I gave a fake shiver.

"Let's go." He motioned to the cabin with the rifle. I moved ahead and toward the door. Toby was on his own.

I pushed open the door, and Guard Guy shoved me in. I stumbled and nearly went headfirst onto the floor, but someone caught me and helped me straighten.

Bruce's expression was grim. "What are you doing here?" His left eye was puffy. His suit wrinkled and dirty.

"What are you doing here?" I replied.

"Sam?" Stella said from behind me.

I turned and rushed to her. "Are you okay?" I scanned her from head to foot. She had a lovely purple bruise at her hairline, above her right temple. Her hair was mussed, her clothes disheveled, and her mascara smudged under her eyes. Either from crying, rubbing them, or both.

"I'm fine. You shouldn't have come," Stella said and hugged me. "I'm so happy to see you, but you shouldn't have come." In my ear, she whispered, "These guys are terrible."

I hugged her back and surveyed the area. The cabin consisted of two rooms. The other likely being a bathroom. The main space had a kitchen along one wall, a couch along the other. Rustic. If used by normal, law-abiding people, this would have likely been a hunting cabin or a space for hikers. But the two goons dressed in black turtlenecks and black slacks, their arms as large as tree trunks folded across their chests, told me hunting animals didn't happen here. They were sporting a few bruises of their own. One had a black eye. Another had a swollen jaw.

I separated from Stella. "I'm guessing you're the Berry Brothers. Which one of you has terrible aim with a rifle?" They were almost identical, subtle differences in the fullness of their faces. But both had dark, piercing eyes.

I randomly pointed to one. "Was it you? You look like a crap shot."

"You mean *crack* shot?" he replied.

"No, I mean crap. I'm standing here, aren't I? And I'm not even armed."

"Sam, don't instigate," Bruce said from behind me.

I turned toward him, and that's when I saw the guy who had to be Prescott. He was my height, brown hair, a boyishly charming face. He could pass for a suburban dad or a teacher. He was dressed in a dark gray suit, which paired with the menacing gleam in his eyes told me his soul was just as dark. He smiled at me, but it looked everything like a sneer and nothing like a grin.

He scanned me up and down, not in a pervy way but more like a machine assessing my weaknesses.

"I came here looking for you," I said to him and took a step in his direction. Swollen-Eye B Brother moved to stand between Prescott and me. He jerked my messenger bag away, nearly ripping my head off.

Prescott said, "Let me apologize for the idiot brothers. You weren't supposed to know you're marked for death. Which is why you're here, right? To make a deal?" He offered me a seat on the couch.

I shook my head. He'd guessed my plan from the start. Kinda took the wind out of my sails. "I'll stand, thank you. So it's true that you took the contract. I want to know if it was just Joe Cooper or Austin Strong, as well, that wanted me dead."

"Why would I tell you anything? How stupid are you to come right to me? As if you have anything to bargain with."

I stared at him. Letting his words hang in the air. Waiting for someone else to make a move of any sort, to let Prescott know I wasn't scared. Even if I was terrified out of my mind. It was the guard at the window who shifted first and looked between me and Prescott.

I said, "Why would I ever think you'd double-cross Joe Cooper? He's a powerful enemy to make. Even if he is in prison. And you're right, what do I have that would be compelling enough to make you do so?" I shook my head. "No, I came because I wanted to let you know I know you're hunting me, and that you'll not get away with any of this."

"I could have you shot right now." He nodded to the guard, who raised his rifle at me.

I crossed my arms and smirked. "Okay, do it." I faced the guard. "Do it."

Bruce groaned. "Shut up, Samantha."

Stella whimpered and collapsed on the couch.

"A million people know that I'm here. Bruce is here. Stella, you, and your henchmen are here. You won't walk out of this unscathed. And I feel pretty confident you take your nearly squeaky-clean arrest record seriously. It's a source of pride for you. But you shoot me, you lose out on two fronts. You don't collect fully on the contract—it's supposed to look like an accident, right? And your record goes to hell. Killing me and these two"—I gestured to Bruce and Stella—"is probably more than your lawyer can sweep under the rug."

Prescott smiled. "I'm not worried."

"I know. That's because you'll throw your goons under

the bus, and they'll do the time. I mean, they will do the actual trigger pulling. Loyalty, it's powerful." I gave the guard a grimace as if to say I was sorry for him. "Too bad he's not loyal to you," I told the guard.

I returned my attention back to Prescott. "But everyone knows you're behind it all. There're other ways to ruin people besides a court trial. I did take down Austin Strong. Remember him? He was enormously more powerful than you. You didn't think I'd come out here without some contingency plan?"

I wasn't sure about the type of man Prescott was. My bluffing could go either way. Either I appealed to his ego with his reputation, or I angered him with the Austin Strong comment. It all depended on Prescott's ego. Would reputation or clout mean more to him?

Prescott eased his hands into his pants pocket. "I know a few things about you, too, Samantha True. Like how much you like the outdoors." To his guard, he said, "Take her outside for a long walk. Don't come back with her. Make it look like an accident."

19

FRIDAY MORNING

HERE'S HOW I SAW IT. LEO KNEW ABOUT THE TRACKER. He knew I was following Bruce. So essentially, he knew where I was. Plus, my folks were going to send him after me. And as a backup plan, I figured Carson was watching me and Prescott if he actually was trying to get to the bottom of this contract. And because Prescott and I were in the same location, I was counting on Carson being around too.

Last, I figured the universe owed me one. Or a few, but out of respect for the universe, I wasn't keeping a running total.

The guard shoved me out of the cabin, his rifle muzzle tapping my back every few steps to keep me moving.

"Where do you want me to go?" Before us was nothing but trees.

"Go to the back of the cabin and start walking away from it and the road."

I needled him out of fear and sheer spite. "That's a dumb idea. Anyone who knows me will know I wouldn't go in this direction. Not if I had come here to the cabin specifically."

"Not my problem," he said.

"Yeah, it kinda is. Because you're gonna be the one who gets hunted down for this and will take the fall. Did you always want to grow up and be a lackey? So much of one, you'd give up your freedom?"

"Shut your pie hole." He jabbed me in the back with the tip of the rifle, hard, forcing me to arch in pain.

"Yow!" I rubbed the spot on my back. We walked in silence for a few beats when the bird call of an American goldfinch came through the trees. Only the pitch was a little off. Not as sweet or high as I was used to.

Leo.

I scanned the trees, looking for a sign. The birdsong came again ahead of me, and I had a general idea in which direction. Putting my hand in front of my chest so the guard couldn't see, I held up four fingers, then did a gun sign. I picked my way through the thick foliage and underbrush heading toward Leo.

I stopped by a large hemlock, so round it was easily six feet in diameter. I faced the guard. "I have to pee."

He rolled his eyes. "Lady, don't you get you're about to die? Peeing shouldn't even be on your radar."

I held up one finger. "But it is. And it's because I know I'm about to die. I don't want to wet my pants. I don't want to soil myself when you go to... you know." I looked pointedly at the gun. "So maybe you could grant this marked-for-death woman one last wish? Please?"

He narrowed his eyes, giving my request some thought. "Apologize for calling me a lackey."

I almost laughed out loud.

Instead, I tried to look remorseful. "Yes, I'm sorry I called you that. I was coming from a place of anger. Now, can I please step behind this tree and do my business?"

He jutted his chin at me, I guess a go-ahead signal.

"I don't suppose you have any toilet paper on you?" I asked.

The guard gave me a weird look. "No, now go before I change my mind."

"Oh, sorry again. I wasn't asking you. I was asking the guy behind you."

Leo had dropped from a tree a few yards back and had crept up on us. Of course, I had the advantage of watching. His Native American heritage and upbringing, paired with all those summers we'd spent in the woods as children, were paying off in spades now. I made a mental note to call Hue and thank him immensely for letting me tag along back then.

The guard must have really thought I was stupid. He glanced over his shoulder, caught sight of Leo standing there, dressed in his cop garb, and jerked in surprise. In three moves, Leo removed the rifle from the guard, shoved his head against a tree, knocking him out, then lowered him to the ground to secure his hands behind his back with flex-cuffs.

"You really are my hero," I said. "I'm so glad to see you."

"I'm glad to see you too. Though it's these situations that I'm hoping to avoid in the future."

"We totally avoided one of those. No bullets were fired. No explosions. The worst is you might have bruised knuckles. I call that a win. Now, I have to get back to the cabin. Bruce is there with Stella, the B Brothers, and Prescott."

Leo pulled me aside and out of earshot of the guard. "Carson is back there. I'll go back to help him. You stay here with this guy. More cops are on their way, but they're behind us by twenty minutes."

"No, I'm not staying here with this guy."

"Someone has to watch him. Don't move him. When he wakes up, just wave the rifle around." He handed me the weapon. It was heavy and awkward in my hands.

A woman screamed, and then a shot rang out in the woods, back in the direction of the cabin.

I whimpered.

"Stay here," Leo said and pointed at the guard as he backpedaled toward the cabin. "Please. Remember, you're a target."

Staying behind was killing me. I faced the guard and waited for him to come to. I paced around him a few times and then sat next to him, setting the rifle to my side, against my leg.

From seemingly out of nowhere, the tip of a gun was pressed to my temple. I stretched my hand out for the rifle.

"Don't move."

It was one of the B Brothers, the one with the swollen jaw. He reached down and snagged the rifle from me. Had the scream been a ruse?

Bruce stumbled out from between the trees and landed on his knees in front of me. His eye had swollen shut and now his lip was cut and his nose was bleeding. They'd beaten him. Swollen-Eye B Brother stepped out behind him.

"Oh, look. It's crap shot."

He held the gun close to my face. "I won't miss this time."

"My friend's emotional-support animal, who doesn't even have opposable thumbs, wouldn't miss at this range." Never mind that I was lying. Sugar gliders had opposable thumbs. But I was tired, and that was the best insult I could come up with for Dumb-Dumb.

He smacked me upside the head with his gun, and for a

second I saw nothing but black, followed by bursting stars in red and yellow. When I opened my eyes, Bruce was sitting next to me, and the guard was being cut from his flex-cuffs.

I blinked a few more times to clear my head. I touched the spot where he'd clocked me, and my hand came away with blood on it.

"We're gonna die, Sam," Bruce said, crying, bloody snot running out his nose.

"No, we aren't."

"It's all my fault, too."

"Well, the Stella part, I'm guessing, is your fault, but them wanting to kill me has nothing to do with you." My ears were ringing, and a headache was bursting free. I couldn't afford a headache. I needed to be free and clear to think. I scooped up some moss and mud, wet and cold with morning dew, and slapped it on the back of my neck. The cold was an instant relief. Then I pressed a large, wet leaf to my temple. I almost sighed out loud. Almost, but I didn't want to draw any attention.

"What did you do to get on Prescott's radar?" Bruce asked.

"I made a rich and powerful man mad. He lost his company and went to prison because of me. What about you?"

Bruce's shoulders shook with sobs. Awkward moments passed before he sucked in a deep breath and said, "I borrowed money from him for some start-ups. Start-ups that failed."

"The vig must be astronomical," I said. Vig was the interest loan sharks put on the money they lent out.

Bruce nodded.

"Why not ask your dad for money?"

"I had, and I'd lost what he gave me, so he refused to give me more. That's when I turned to Prescott."

"Did he do that to your trigger finger?"

Bruce held up his hand, the index finger permanently extended. "Yeah."

"That looks like it was a while ago." I was trying to connect the dots. How long had Bruce and Prescott been doing business?"

"While I was on the force. I had to take an early retirement. Thankfully, I had the years in."

"You were in cahoots with Prescott while you were on the force?" I couldn't keep the accusation out of my voice.

He hung his head in what I could only hope was shame.

"How did we get here, Bruce? With Stella kidnapped and you looking down the barrel of a gun?"

"I'm a two-time loser, Sam. That's how we got here. I failed at being a cop, and I failed at being a businessman, and I made deals with bad people." He started crying again. "My dad has lost so much, and now he's going to lose more and it's my fault."

Well, if he was taking responsibility, that was one redeeming quality. "But why would Prescott take Stella? Why was he trying to shake down your dad?"

I get Bruce owed and owed big. But why would Prescott go after Bruce's dad? Sure, it was easy enough to find out Tom had the money, but why not snatch Bruce?

Then it hit me. Because Tom probably wouldn't pay for Bruce. Wow, Prescott was ruthless. He would get his money any way he could.

"You owe Prescott three million?"

He shook his head. "Two and a half."

Swollen-Eye B Brother walked over and aimed the gun

at Bruce. "Why don't you tell her the rest? Get it off your chest. I hear confession is good for the soul. Maybe you might go to heaven instead of hell."

Bruce shook his head, full-out sobbing now.

"Tell me what?" I asked Swollen Eye.

"How he was gonna kidnap the lady and ransom her. That's how he planned to pay off his debt."

In that moment, the pieces clicked together. "He was going to use Sticks and Stone to do it, right?"

Swollen Eye rolled his eyes, then groaned, wincing. "Those two goofs. They remind me of someone."

"Those idiots in that Christmas movie about the kid whose parents leave him behind?" Toby had said the same thing. Swollen Eye laughed. "Yeah, that's the one."

"*Home Alone?* Others have said the same thing."

"Yeah, that's the one."

I laughed. "That's a pretty appropriate description. One of them mooned me."

"They're how we found you on that back road. Turned you in."

"I figured as much. Owe you money, do they?"

Swollen Eye grinned.

The guard was still on the ground, rubbing his hands and stretching his arms. He was moving slowly. I knew where he was coming from, having taken a blow to the head myself.

"See, Bruce," Swollen Eye said. "No one will know that you sold out your family, but you can go to your grave with a clean slate."

I chuckled. "I don't think he's that lucky. He'll probably live," I said. "Do you mind if I stand? My legs are cramping."

Swollen Eye narrowed his eyes at me. "Don't do anything funny."

"Nope, don't have anything funny in me." I rubbed my temple. "This knocked it right out of me." I eased up, crawling my hands up my legs to show them how weak and unstable I was, how much support I needed. When I was upright, I stretched one arm out to the tree and swayed. "Whoa, maybe standing was a bad idea." I put a hand to my mouth.

Bruce had stopped crying and was scurrying away. "Don't puke on me."

I shook my head and made my eyes go wide to show that moving my head had been a bad idea.

"Oh no, I'm a sympathetic vomiter," said the guard. "Watching her is making me sick."

"I shouldn't have had those eggs for breakfast," I said.

"Go behind the tree," Swollen Jaw said to me through clenched teeth. "Hurry."

I moved unsteadily around the tree, swaying and holding my stomach, adding in dry heaving sounds every few steps. When I got around the tree, I made like I was emptying my stomach. It was kinda hard as I didn't have any liquid to splash around, but I rustled the leaves and threw some dirt at the ground. I spit a few times for good measure. I could only hope my improvising would work.

From the other side of the tree, the guard said, "I'm gonna be sick."

I continued with my "vomiting," hoping to trigger him. The nausea hadn't been too hard to fake when I stood, but that had faded.

"Here it comes," the guard cried. Immediately, upchucking sounds filled the air.

"Oh, that's making *me* sick," Bruce said. "It smells so rank."

"Don't get it on my shoe," One of the B Brothers yelled.

I peeked around the tree. Guard Guy was on his knees, bent over, kissing the ground. Swollen Jaw had put the gun down and taken off his shoe, attempting to wipe it with a leaf.

I stepped from around the tree, walked up to the bent-over Swollen Jaw and said, "Hi."

He looked up at me, unfazed. That's when I kicked him in the crotch. Hard. He bent further at the waist and turned green, groaning.

And because I couldn't take any chances—this was life or death after all—I grabbed him by the ears, held tight, and headbutted him with all my might, smashing his nose in the process. I staggered back, stunned, but only slightly.

The good thing about being the headbutter and not the headbuttee was that it hurt less. Still hurt, but less. And I figured I was going to have a headache anyway.

He fell to the ground. I snatched up the rifle and brought the blunt end down on his head, knocking out his lights.

The guard stood, confused. Wiping his mouth.

"I can shoot you or you can comply. I'm leaning toward shooting," I said.

Behind him, Leo and three other cops were breaking through the trees.

He put his hands in the air. "I surrender. Lady, you're one helluva jinx or something."

I smiled. "Thanks."

20

A WEEK LATER

STELLA AND TOM WERE MARRIED. SAME VENUE, SAME wedding planner. Only this time, Leo was the best man as Bruce was in jail. Along with Prescott, the B Brothers and the guard, whose name I found out was John Johnson. With a name as unoriginal as that, no wonder he went toward a life of crime.

No one had shown up at the drop. Bruce had told Prescott the FBI was involved.

Stella had been unhurt, except for when the ski-mask man, one of the B Brothers, had snatched her and knocked her out. Her deepest wound had come from Bruce's betrayal.

Jessica was at the wedding too, her triplets now four days old. She stood next to me as we represented Stella. We both wore dresses in a soft pink, but in cuts that flattered our bodies. I'd asked the seamstress to put pockets on my dress, and though she'd looked at me like I was crazy, she had. Pockets were a girl's best friend.

Leo and I stood along a wall at the reception and

watched others dance and laugh. Leo handed me the tracker he'd given me.

"Do you still want this?"

"Yes, are you kidding? This handy-dandy gadget saved my life." I slipped it into the dress pocket, where it rested against my mini stun gun.

A girl couldn't be too cautious.

"I know Prescott's in jail, but that doesn't mean the contract's going away," Leo said.

"Nope, which means Carson won't be going away anytime soon either."

For what it was worth, I couldn't begrudge that. Carson had been the first person Precious had encountered when she'd left the woods that day. He'd been heading toward us, having put a tracker on Precious's SUV as well. Toby had met them at the road and told them the latest. He and Carson had headed to the cabin, leaving Precious to bring Leo up to speed when he'd arrived minutes later. Carson had made it to the cabin after one of the B Brothers had left to take care of Bruce and had come upon me and the guard. Carson had rescued Stella.

So with this contract still active, I'd happily take any additional eyes watching my back. Even if they were Carson's.

"So do we have to pretend to be engaged until he leaves?" Leo dropped an arm across my shoulder.

"He's been watching us already and bought the story, so I figure we can be like normal. Besides, it's not like he's going to be telling anyone. He's trying to stay dead." Thankfully, we hadn't had to share the video of Carson with the FBI. I looked over Leo's shoulder. "Heads-up, Mariah is headed this way."

Leo tossed back his glass of champagne. Then did the same with mine.

"For strength or courage? I asked.

"Both," he said. "She scares me."

"Leo," Mariah called out, extending her arms wide. "We didn't get to spend any time together. Sadly, though, I can't stay."

"It was good seeing you, Mariah," he said.

She pulled him into a hug, forcing him to take his arm off my shoulder. He stood stiffly as she wiggled against him.

"It was just so great to see you." She stepped away and ran a hand down his cheek while batting her extended lashes at him.

To me, she said, "I hear we have you to thank for all this, Samantha." She gestured to the roomful of people. "That there wouldn't have been a wedding without you. You saved the day."

"No, that's not true. I had a hunch that panned out. Leo, a friend, and some other cops saved the day."

She made a pouty face. "Well, don't worry, the rumor mill is you saved everyone. No one needs to know the truth. Run with it."

I didn't have a response because I wasn't sure how to take what she said. I stuck my hands in my pockets and fidgeted with the items there.

"Oh," I said, suddenly struck with inspiration. "I'm not worried. I got to use my stun gun." I pulled the mini out of my pocket. "And I knocked a guy out with the butt of a rifle. I'm feeling pretty good about things." I flipped the cover off the stun gun, exposing the prongs. "Want to see how this works?"

Mariah gave a fake laugh. "You are so cute. And perfect

for him." She patted Leo's chest. "Who knew he liked his women so tough."

I thought about all the girls he'd asked out. I raised my hand. "Me. I knew. That's his type. It's not hair color, skin color, or height. It's resiliency. Self-reliance. That's what he likes."

Leo smiled at me and slid his arm back over my shoulder.

"Funny, for a couple engaged to get married, I haven't really seen any public displays of affection between you two." Mariah tapped her nose. "Curious."

"We're private people," Leo said.

I moved out from under his arm and stepped in front of him. I grabbed his suit jacket at the chest with both hands and pulled him closer. "We are private people," I said, looking into his eyes. "But sometimes some things just can't wait until the door is closed."

"Like right now?" he asked with a smile.

"Yeah, like right now. You ready for this?"

"I'm all in," he said in a low, husky voice.

"Me too." I pulled him closer.

"I always have been," he said seconds before I pressed my lips to his.

Boy howdy, that man can kiss.

READY FOR THE next Samantha True? It's in the works. In the mean time, you have two options:

1. You can check out Campus Murder Club. That's an episodic story told on Amazon's Vella. Go there and catch the first few episodes free.

2. Or Check out Perfect Place. I've included the first chapter here. It's written under my pen name Robbie Peale. Enjoy.

A LIARS ISLAND SUSPENSE

PERFECT
PLACE

ROBBIE PEALE

HOUR 1

4:10 p.m.

CORA KINCAID PRESSED THE REMOTE-ACCESS BUTTON clipped to her car's visor to open the gate to her housing community. Sprawling mansions spread across the upscale community on Liars Island. With large lots, manicured yards, and hired staff to maintain all of it, Paradox Coves Estates was, contrary to its name, perfect.

Her house, a three-car-garage Tudor, was waiting for her in a cul-de-sac at the end of Perfect Place Drive.

Cora was glad to be home at the end of a long week. All she wanted was to spend some time with her daughter, Ellie, and husband, Sawyer. Maybe they would go to the beach or take the ferry to Seattle for a quick visit to the aquarium and dinner out.

She turned into the neighborhood and glanced in the rearview mirror, checking to see if anybody was following her in. One imperfect thing about her housing community was that other cars without access codes could follow behind those who did have them. That had happened before. Typically, however, they were friends or family of Cora's neighbors and not anyone untoward. But one couldn't be too careful.

Before turning right, toward her street, Cora checked for traffic. To her left, Ann Marie Collins was having groceries delivered. An Eco Landscaping truck was to her right, parked at the corner diagonally from Cora. A handful of landscapers were maintaining the residences' lawns and the common areas.

To Cora's right the street was quiet. She was distracted when her cell phone rang.

The number popped up on the large center dashboard in her beloved Mercedes-Benz G-Class. She took pride in the SUV being the only dark-green vehicle in the neighborhood, a custom order and birthday gift from her husband the previous year.

Recognizing the number as one from her office, she clicked the Answer button on her steering wheel.

She was almost home, yet work was not letting her go.

"This is Cora."

"Hi, Cora. It's Bob." Dr. Robert Schneider was one of the psychiatrists she worked with at Compassion Counseling.

As a marriage and family counselor, Cora loved her job and coworkers. When some clients needed more than she could offer, she knew, when referring them to a psychiatrist in her office, that her clients were getting the best.

"Hi, Dr. Bob, it's almost closing time. Why are you still there?"

She glanced at the dashboard clock: ten after four.

Ellie had arrived home from school forty minutes before, and the agreement she had with her husband, Sawyer, was that he closed his laptop precisely when Eleanor came in the door. That's when family time began. That's what she taught at Compassion Counseling and what she practiced at home.

Dr. Bob chuckled. "That's why I'm calling. I'd like to catch the four-thirty ferry if I can. Miriam is meeting me in Seattle for drinks, dinner, and theater. But I have a client on my books, a Lisa Boynton, but she hasn't shown for her four o'clock appointment. I was wondering if she was chronically late and whether I should wait."

Cora groaned. Convincing Lisa to see Dr. Bob had taken months, and she'd missed her first appointment.

Cora said, "No, she's typically on time. If she's not there by now, then she's not coming. I'll follow up with her on Monday. I knew she was nervous about seeing another provider, but I thought I'd managed to make her comfortable with it. I guess I overestimated my powers of persuasion. Or underestimated her fear. Thanks for waiting, Dr. Bob."

He said, "Maybe do one more appointment with her, and I'll come meet her. Try to make her more comfortable with the switch."

Cora said, "That would be wonderful. Now, go catch that ferry."

They exchanged quick goodbyes as Cora cruised toward her home.

A plain white delivery van, the kind with a high top and no windows on the sides, passed as it left her street. No company logo adorned the side, but vans like that were commonplace. Somewhere on Perfect Place Drive, someone had a package waiting on their doorstep if it hadn't been put directly into their hands.

Typically, Cora didn't pay attention to such service vehicles, but those white vans were a hot topic among the moms on Liars Island. Only the day before on the Islanders in the Know Facebook page, a poster Cora didn't know had gone on a rant about limiting access to those vans and even created a petition.

That was all born of a horrible story from Seattle in which a twelve-year-old was abducted from a park, never to be seen again and likely lost to the underworld of human trafficking. The only clue was a white delivery van last seen near the child. With Seattle being just a ferry ride away, the story had felt too close to home.

Over the past month, the majority of the posts in the group were about how the vans needed to be monitored when they came onto the island. The mommas did not like the free access and unaccountability the vans had. Many moms sincerely believed the vans were trolling neighborhoods for nefarious reasons, to kidnap children from Liars Island for human trafficking. Cora thought if anything criminal was going on, it was likely that porch pirates were waiting around to steal delivered packages. Yet the moms would get spun up by a few smartly worded posts, mostly written by people Cora didn't know, that pushed the fear button, and all hell would break loose... online.

Chuckling at the absurdity of it all, she waved to the unknowingly profiled van driver as he passed. The windows were tinted, and a person would have to strain to make out the driver, but Cora had no interest checking the person out. Statistically speaking, the odds of that van driving through her neighborhood with the intent to kidnap a child was insanely low.

Cora didn't take human trafficking lightly, and she didn't think bad things never happened on Liars Island. She just knew the hysteria of one mom could drive the other moms to the same heights. Logic and reason weren't a consideration in the conversation. A productive conversation about the concern, with solutions, couldn't be had due to all the emotions. That's what irritated Cora the most: the mob mentality that all vans and their drivers were bad until proven otherwise.

She pulled her Mercedes into her drive, deciding not to park inside the garage because she was going to take Ellie out for ice cream.

Exiting her vehicle with her purse and briefcase, she glanced at the rare blue and sunny sky. The spring weather was a perfect mid-seventies with the sun having followed a quick drizzle. The change in season was driving Cora's need to get outside and enjoy the sun. The winter had been long and full of gray skies common to the Pacific Northwest.

At the front door, Cora picked up a package leaning against her door. The white van had apparently delivered a box from Amazon.

If Cora were to guess, the contents were likely Ellie's much anticipated slime-making kit. Her eight-year-old had saved four weeks of chore money to buy it. Waiting the two days for its arrival had almost killed her.

Cora grabbed the box and tucked it under an arm, then keyed in the house code that unlocked the front door.

After stepping inside, she placed her bags and the box on the large foyer table and called out, "Hello, I'm home. Where are you two?"

The house was unusually quiet, considering Ellie was typically famished after arriving home from school, and Sawyer would usually be chatting with her about her day while making her a snack.

"Hello?"

She moved from the foyer to the hall that looked down to the kitchen. The room was empty. She stopped at the base of the stairs.

A noise in the hall at the top of the stairs drew her attention. Moments later, Sawyer came into sight. His curly hair was pushed off his forehead from hours of resting his forehead in his hand, which he tended to do when in thought. His glasses sat low on his nose, and his shirtsleeves were rolled up, a pen behind one ear.

"Hello, love. You're home early." Tracking time was not Sawyer's strong suit as he had a tendency to get lost in his writing, and ever since he'd lost his personal assistant, he'd required built-in reminders such as alarm clocks. But he also needed reminders to set his alarm clocks, and Cora had forgotten to do that before she'd left this morning.

He continued, "You've beaten Ellie home. Hang on a sec, and I'll come down. We can wait outside together for the bus."

A cold wave of something foreign and unfamiliar washed over Cora—maybe fear.

"Sawyer, Ellie should be home by now. It's after four." As she spoke, she backpedaled toward the door.

Sawyer shook his head. "But she hasn't come home. I've been waiting for her to come in. That's my cue to stop writing."

Cora took a deep breath. A logical explanation had to exist. Ellie was in the TV room. Or her room. Or talking with her friend next door. But she knew not to do that.

"Ellie!" Cora called.

Nothing. Waiting for a response was agony.

Cora jerked the door open and stepped outside. She

looked up and down the quiet street. No movement. No cars coming home. No children outside playing. No Ellie.

She went back inside. "She's not out there."

Sawyer said, "I'll look up here—you down there. Then we'll call the school to see if the bus is running late."

Cora wondered what the likelihood of that was. Her heart raced.

———

THIS FAST PACED story is a 2-4 hour read and will leave you breathless. Grab Perfect Place now!

LET'S KEEP IN TOUCH

I hope you enjoy this book. I'd love to connect and share more with you. Sign up to receive emails about and other goodies..

There, I'll share all sorts of book information. You'll be the first to know about my sales and new releases. You'll have access to giveaways, freebies, and bonus content. Think you might be interested? Give me a try. You can always leave at any time.

DID YOU ENJOY THIS BOOK?

If so...

As football kicker Pat McAfee says: **Be a friend, tell a friend.**

You can also leave a review: Click to review

Lend it , Recommend it , Review it

XO, Kristi

MEET KRISTI ROSE

Hey! I'm Kristi. I write romances that will tug your heartstrings and laugh out loud mysteries. In all my stories you'll fall in love with the cast of characters, they'll become old, fun friends. **My one hope** is that I create stories that *satisfy any of your book cravings* and take you away from the rut of everyday life (sometimes it's a good rut).

When I'm not writing I'm spinning (riding a stationary bike), repurposing Happy Planners, or drinking a London Fog (hot tea with frothy milk).

I'm the mom of 2 and a milspouse (retired). We live in the Pacific Northwest and are under-prepared if one of the volcanoes erupts.

Here are 3 things about me:

- I lived on the outskirts of an active volcano (Mt.Etna)
- A spider bit me and it laid eggs in my arm (my kids don't know that story yet)
- I grew up in Central Florida and have skied in lakes with gators.

I'd love to get to know you better. Join my Read & Relax

community and then fire off an email and tell me 3 things about you!

Not ready to join? Email me below or follow me at one of the links below. Thanks for popping by!

You can connect with Kristi at any of the following:
www.kristirose.net
kristi@kristirose.net

CPSIA information can be obtained
at www.ICGtesting.com
Printed in the USA
LVHW081939120122
708420LV00016B/1401